Rich thought a second before asking, "Are you really ready to die?"

"Who said I was ready?"

"You did."

"Okay. So what if I am?" Jenny pushed her tray away. "Obviously, most people are ready to die."

"Why?"

"Look at Stop the Nightmare. Out of all the people in Montana—in the whole country—how many care one way or another about the nuclear thing?"

Rich shrugged. "Not many."

"And what about you?"

"Me?" He wanted to get the words, the thoughts right. But instead, he just said what he was thinking. "I don't care that much about dying. Everybody dies. But I don't want everybody to die at once. That's a nightmare. The sun rising one morning, and all the people are gone. That's what it means to me."

"Yeah. But how far will you go to fight it?"

Rich didn't know how to answer that.

Jenny said, "I think there's only one person around here who wants to live bad enough to really do anything about it. That's Max."

Max? For a split second Rich felt . . . What? Jealous? That was crazy. Max was someone with important things ahead of him. It was only right that Jenny should admire him. Still . . .

Jenny brushed her hair back. "Well, we can talk all we want, but we need to start doing things."

"Like what?"

"Max will know."

THE TWENTY-SIX MINUTES

Robert Hawks

Square One Publishers, Inc.
Madison, Wisconsin

A Stamp Out Sheep Press Book

Library of Congress Cataloging-in-Publication Data

Hawks, Robert.
The twenty-six minutes / Robert Hawks.
p.   cm. — (A Stamp Out Sheep Press book)

Summary: Two teenagers, children of career Air Force
officers, become involved in a disarmament group and in
the life of its charismatic leader.
ISBN 0-938961-03-9 : $4.95
[1. Nuclear disarmament—Fiction.]   I. Title.   II. Title: 26
minutes.
PZ7.H313545Tw 1988

88-11454
CIP
AC

Design: David McLimans
Cover Photo: James Gill

First printing July 1988
Manufactured in the United States of America

For Mark Brooks

THE FIRST PART

GREYLAKE, MONTANA
population: 71, 440
Home of the 633rd Strategic Missile
Wing . . . 200 Nuclear Missiles on 24
hour a day standby alert . . .
Since 1962.

sign posted at Travers AFB gate:
STRATEGIC AIR COMMAND—*PEACE IS
OUR PROFESSION.*

ANNOUNCEMENT!!!

BEYOND THE NUCLEAR FREEZE—
"SAVE THE CHILDREN"

Stop the Nightmare demands that the United States of America dismantle and neutralize one—just one—Minuteman missile in the name of world peace. Once we have set the precedent, the Soviets will have no choice but to follow our lead. This bold initiative will incite an avalanche of world opinion. The genie **can** be put back into the bottle. The peace movement **must** begin in our own backyard.

STN NEEDS YOU!

An organizational meeting will be held at the Civic Center, downtown Greylake, Thursday November Fourteenth at Eight P.M.

We can save the children, but we need **your** help!

One

"All of us here in this room are no more than twenty-six minutes away from death."

Jenny Westphal jumped at that. She had expected a horror story from the guest speaker, but nothing so direct. Jenny was sitting at her desk near the back radiator of the sociology classroom. The reason she had not expected anything so direct was because the classroom was in the high school on Travers Air Force Base, and generally the kids on the base were kept sheltered from bad thoughts like that. Jenny shrugged it off and kept doodling. The notebook paper binder she was writing on was new. Her first notebook of the year, scrawled repeatedly with variations on the name Kirk Mowry, had been recently discarded.

"Everyone in Greylake, Montana today is targeted."

Doesn't this guy let up, Jenny wondered. She shrunk a bit in her chair when she caught a glimpse of his eyes. Falcon's eyes, a bird seeking prey. The speaker's name was Maxwell Neuger. A fair-complexioned young man of about twenty-five, he was lean but rumpled looking in a baggy blue sweater and jeans. Jenny squinted, and decided that his face was *irregular*. His nose was too pointed, his cheeks too high, and his forehead too proud.

The eyes were different, though. They blazed. They seemed to accuse everyone in the room of some grisly crime.

Or maybe, Jenny thought, those eyes see things that aren't really there.

3

Maxwell Neuger was—in the words of her father, Captain Daddy—"the anti-nuclear nut from Michigan." He stared directly at her for a second, and she dropped lower in her seat. It was the crazy and easy reaction, and if there were two things Jenny felt comfortable with, they were the crazy and easy ways out of situations. Neuger's stare was more scary than anything he said. His voice was soothing, almost ironic. "If a Soviet missile were to airburst over this school right now, everything for five square miles would be vaporized. What this means is that all of the water which comprises your bodies—and that is more than ninety-six percent of what you are made of—all of that water would be instantly converted to steam."

He snapped his fingers. "You wouldn't even be aware of what was happening. Oh, you might sense a bright flash of light, but probably not. By the time your optic nerve could transmit the flash of light to your brain, all of that brain matter will have already been vaporized. It will happen that fast."

He paused for effect. "Should you be so lucky."

Jenny felt a chill. The class was totally quiet, waiting, and it was frightening. She could see why Captain Daddy had nearly refused to sign the permission slip to allow her to see the film and listen to the speaker. Jenny had assumed he was being ignorant. He was in the Air Force and didn't like his daughter hearing anything controversial about it. Maybe that wasn't the reason after all. She had to admit that Maxwell Neuger was persuasive. More than persuasive.

He was hypnotic.

Jenny had read about people who could hypnotize with a gaze. Like Adolf Hitler or the killer Charles Manson. They could look into your eyes and make you believe things that weren't true. Jenny had never heard of anyone good being able to do it.

Suddenly, she felt disoriented, lost in time. Okay, Wednesday, she thought. The guest speaker was coming Wednesday, and there he was, so it had to be Wednesday. The day was getting rather recurrent. Lately it seemed to be hitting on the average of once a week.

4

Neuger still spoke. "For the unlucky millions who survive that dreadful instant, the worst will be yet to come. Millions who are terribly burned will find almost no doctors. Ninety-eight percent of America's medical resources lie within what are considered primary target zones. Nearly all the foodstuffs will be hopelessly contaminated. The water table will be poisoned. Death by gruesome radiation sickness . . . inevitable." Neuger cocked his head at Patty Myer, who jumped. Patty was one of Jenny's best friends, and the Wing Commander's daughter. She wondered if Neuger knew that. Was that why he gave Patty the look?

This bothered Jenny. Nothing flustered Patty. Now she looked as if she had been slapped. Patty avoided Neuger's gaze; instead, she stared at the mural engraved across her desk.

That wasn't right. Patty upset by a guest speaker? Marcie's dad was probably right in not allowing her to listen. If Patty was rattled, Marcie would have been in tears. Her dad, a Captain in one of the missile squadrons, had called Maxwell Neuger a subversive and refused to sign the parental permission slip. Still, Jenny felt a little bad about Marcie not being there. She had been the first person Jenny had met at the Travers Air Force Base High School, and she was still, along with Patty, one of her best friends. Even if she was sometimes too excitable.

Neuger continued. "It takes a Soviet missile warhead, journeying through outer space over the North Pole, just twenty-six minutes to travel from its launch pad to any target in the United States." With his finger he made an arc over the globe of the world which he had been hugging through most of his lecture. "This is mankind's greatest technological achievement. No one in the world is more than twenty-six minutes away from burning to death."

Jenny closed her eyes. She wondered if anybody else in the world was sitting back, also wondering if anybody else in the world was feeling this lousy. She tried to project her thoughts out to wherever and whoever that person might be: *Feel not alone.*

The day had begun borderline for Jenny and was slip-

5

ping fast. She kept her eyes closed and her mind as blank as possible for a few seconds, on the off chance that there might be a reply.

No answer.

Jenny opened her eyes. Such was life.

Maxwell Neuger was still speaking. He was staring hard at everyone in class now, daring them just to sit there and continue breathing normally. He did it with his gaze. "Imagine it now," he said. "Rising in a pillar of flame and smoke from its silo deep in the Ukraine. Climbing skyward, dropping its first stage. America naked before it, unaware. The people, that is. The children. The military machinery will be clattering, alarm bells ringing, coded messages flashing. The second stage is blown free and the missile begins to arc its way over the pole. Twenty-six minutes is a long time. Plenty of time to prime our own retaliation, launch our own missiles. They're around here, you know. In Montana. In backyards and fields. You'll see them blast away; you'll know it's started. But what will you do in that twenty-six minutes? What will you do as the third and final stage of that Soviet rocket separates from the warhead? What will you do as the hydrogen bomb screams down at you at ten times the speed of sound? Towards you. Towards your city, your family, your friends, as that first great flash of awesome light envelops—"

A chair was knocked back suddenly. Neuger stopped speaking as Robin Howard stood and left the classroom. The door closed quietly behind her. Neuger watched her go, then turned to stare again at the rest of the class. He didn't speak for a moment; he just stared.

Jenny met his eyes this time and held his gaze. She felt jumpy and nervesick. She wondered if there was any power in her own eyes. She was a pale girl, thin, with deeply-set dark eyes and very high cheekbones. Long, stringy black hair edged her face and fell in bangs across her forehead. Captain Daddy said it made her look like a throwback to the 1960's, but that wasn't very likely since she was only seventeen years old. She sat up abruptly in her seat and leaned forward on the flat desk.

She knew in an instant that if she looked long enough into those eyes she would see through them. But Neuger turned away. She didn't have time.

Jenny could hear just then the very small voice inside her, the voice that usually spoke only at home when Captain Daddy and her stepmother, the Cockroach Woman, performed another episode of "Why Did We Ever Get Married, Anyway?" The voice inside Jenny begged for quiet, but never out loud. She didn't want to involve herself in the fights, didn't want to become part of the seemingly endless name-calling. Occasionally, the voice inside would gather itself up into a tiny ball, drawing smaller. One day it would disappear entirely, and Jenny worried about that day. The pressure was unbearable sometimes, especially when Captain Daddy came home from the missile field. He was posted for twenty-four hours at a time, and when he returned, the Cockroach Woman usually found something to jump on him for. It was as if Jenny had a vise on her head, with the Cockroach Woman taking a turn and then Captain Daddy and then the Cockroach Woman and then . . .

This was different, though. The voice inside was not concerned with Captain Daddy or the Cockroach Woman. It was concerned with Maxwell Neuger. It was upset because there hadn't been enough time to see into his eyes. Why did it care? There was probably nothing special in those eyes, anyway. Nothing new.

Now there was a question, thought Jenny. Was there ever really anything new? Do we ever really tread new ground? Or do we just occasionally become lost in the familiar?

So much for the voice.

Maxwell Neuger was finishing up. "Can you live with this?" he asked. "Can you live in the shadow of the twenty-six minutes for the rest of your lives? If you feel that you can, fine. But if you are like myself and millions of others around the world then you are coming to realize that this circus sideshow cannot go on. But until our national leaders recognize that the American people no longer wish to be used as nuclear bargaining chips, absolutely nothing will happen.

"Except maybe a nuclear holocaust."

Neuger shook his head. "It is almost midnight, folks. The clock is winding down. We still have a little time to act, but not all that much. We cannot continue to debate the issue. What we need now is positive action. And that is what the Stop the Nightmare group stands for.

"Remember the twenty-six minutes."

He set the globe down in the center of the classroom floor and backed away from it. At first everyone in class seemed to hesitate, then a nervous, unsure applause began to break out. Maggie Flynn was the first to applaud, others joined in, and Jenny even found herself clapping. Mr. Bradley, the sociology teacher who had arranged the entire affair, got up to shake Neuger's hand. He was mumbling something which Jenny strained to hear but couldn't make out. She was still watching Neuger's eyes.

They were not on fire anymore, she decided. They just looked tired and sad. It was as if he realized that he was going to keep travelling and speaking but in the end he was still going to die in the same nuclear fireball that consumed everyone. The kids from the class were beginning to crowd around and ask questions, but Jenny thought Maxwell Neuger looked very much alone.

How many people feel so alone, she wondered. Everyone, or just the world's selected lonely types? Jenny placed herself in this category and gave Maxwell Neuger a spot on that shelf as well. Again, she directed her thoughts toward that other miserable person in the world: One and one and another make three.

She tugged down the bottom of her sweatshirt and frowned. The shirt read RAPID CITY SEEGAR JUNIOR HIGH SCHOOL and was a holdover from her South Dakota days when Captain Daddy had been Lieutenant Daddy and was still married to Barbara, Jenny's mother. They had been stationed then at Ellsworth Air Force Base, just outside of Rapid City. That was the story of her life, Jenny thought. Always destined to be "just outside" of someplace.

In a panic, she sniffed back a wetness that had appeared without warning on her face. She chilled a bit and looked around. Nobody had noticed; everyone was intent on Neuger. Button down, she thought. No tears, no scenes. Otherwise you'll find yourself being shipped back to Dr. Pipps for a full refund.

Okay, she appealed to that other miserable person in the world. Where do we go from here?

Still no answer.

Jenny looked back to Maxwell Neuger. She was the only one in class still seated now. He seemed to notice this and looked her way, but only for a second. As far as the nuclear thing went, Jenny thought it all frightening, but there was probably nothing anyone could do. She was tired of hearing about it. Being the daughter of an Air Force Captain stationed at a missile base, she was subjected to more of it than most. She hadn't really been interested in seeing the film *First Strike!* or hearing the lecture until she discovered a parental permission slip was required. Hearing that, she assumed something spicy was involved. So why not?

Jenny decided to play it down when she spoke to Marcie as promised. She wouldn't look for her right away. First she would go home and be nice to her stepbrother, Wesley. She would even be nice to the Cockroach Woman, if at all possible. She would feed her fish, the red bettas she adored, and clean the algae from the tank if necessary. Maybe she would even write her mother. Only then would she call Marcie.

One thing was certain. When she talked to Marcie, she would leave out the part about Maxwell Neuger's eyes. She would have to deal with his eyes in her own way, in either a letter to Mom, a poem, or a note. Probably not a letter; she was writing Mom way too much these days. A poem seemed a good idea; it was a very poetic image, burning eyes. Wait. *Hephaestus* eyes, Hephaestus being the Greek god of fire. Sounded good, but Jenny had no confidence in her poetry, so it would probably be a note. Jenny steeled herself. Yes, it would definitely be a note. Which was weird, and more than a little unusual maybe, but Jenny didn't keep a proper journal, and her suicide notes were the closest thing to a diary that she had . . .

9

Two

Something unusual was happening.

It wasn't unusual for a fight to be taking place in the empty lot across the street from the base high school. That was almost a daily occurence, as if the lot had been placed there especially for fighting. Nor was it really unusual for Rich McFadden to be standing there, about to be mashed to a pulp. That was not quite a daily occurence, but it happened often enough. Actually, there was not all that much unusual about the scene at all, except . . .

Except that Rich hadn't flipped yet.

He stood there rigid, clutching his books, still quite calm though his cheek was burning red from the slap he had just received from Longhair. Longhair was a truly freaky-looking kid in tattered blue jeans and a red flannel work shirt. He had a mane of long, frizzy, dirty blond hair, and one of his yellowing front teeth was chipped.

He was taunting Rich, digging at him. "Come on," he said. "Come on and hit me back, *boy*." Longhair grinned then, emphasizing the word *boy* for those friends of his who were standing there watching. A couple of freshmen kicked at the dirt, happy not to be in Rich's shoes.

Should sell tickets to these events, thought Rich. Print programs. Set up concession stands. That's the real problem here: These fights are never properly scheduled. If we could just preannounce—

Longhair slapped Rich again. He seemed to want Rich to fight back. All of the right people were gathering around to watch, and it was reputation time. If Rich would just try and hit him back—any futile effort would do—it would provide the excuse needed to go ahead and slam him. Not that an excuse was needed.

Rich was having none of it. Still no reaction.

He was thinking one word: No.

The next slap, which was so fast that one could hardly follow it, knocked Rich's glasses off. Frowning, Rich stood there silently taking it. He could see something in Longhair's eyes that no one else could—a distant look, almost of insanity.

What was the line?

Oh, yeah.

Someday we'll all laugh over this—

Slap.

Rich held his gaze. Eye contact. Wasn't that what the gym teacher always said? Never let your opponent see you turn away. Never avoid the eye of the serpent.

Unless, of course, he's a lot bigger than you.

The crowd of students around them was growing now, many of them wandering over from the bus stop in order to watch Longhair destroy Rich. No other outcome was conceivable. Longhair, never one to disappoint an audience, much less the friends who were cheering him on, started to toss combinations at Rich. "Come on!" he screamed. Two quick slaps. Another. The next was almost a punch. "Come on, *boy*!"

What came next was almost certainly a punch, connecting to Rich's jaw with a sickening thud.

Still no reaction.

Rich wondered what the future held for guys like Longhair. Meaningful careers, where they could stand tall asking that contemplative question, "Would you like fries with that, ma'am?"

He said nothing, though. In fact, that was the problem. Because inside, way inside, that strange pressure was building. The weird thoughts kept coming. A Rich McFadden flip-out was possible at any time.

The crowd of students knew it. They were milling about and chatting, excited by the struggle—two gladiators? one

11

and a half gladiators?—but at the same time oblivious to it.

The fight was irrelevant.

The real show might begin any moment.

The one-sided battle was enraging Longhair. He was punching rapidly and shouting now. "Come on!"

Rich was playing statues.

Highly unusual.

Unusual because in most cases, Rich would have flipped by this point. Which is not to say that he would have retaliated with a series of well-timed blows, disabling his opponent—far from it. Rich didn't fight. His reactions were always unpredictable; the kid in the wire-rimmed glasses had yet to repeat himself. The reason for all of the giggly talk around school was simple: When confronted, Rich tended to weird out. Weird out? Rich was amazed by that. What could possibly be weirder than fighting, than hurting people? Obviously one thing was— the son of an Air Force Non-Commissioned Officer refusing to lift a hand to defend himself. Accepting punishment calmly, without reply. That was like that guru guy in India, what was his name? Gandhi? Yeah. Look what happened to him. He got shot.

Good God, now he was comparing himself to Gandhi. Making a bit much of everything, wasn't he? Not unusual. Whenever someone picked a fight with Rich, he could never tell whether Rich was going to follow him home afterwards as a silent reminder, or sit on the ground, trying to tell the story of the Washita Valley, where hundreds of Indians were massacred by the troops of General George Armstrong Custer. The word was out. Rich was good, honest fun. Provided you had the time for it.

Longhair apparently had the time for it. About thirty kids circled them now, giving plenty of room. Longhair grinned, ready for action. Rich tried to stay calm. He could feel the blood vessels in his nose on the verge of bursting. Terrific. Not now, he thought. Please not—

A punch to the cheek wrenched him from a thought. Please—

12

Another punch.

—Don't do anything stupid, don't do—

A head popping

—anything stupid, your whole life's been—

sickening

—PLEASE DON'T DO ANYTHING STUPID!

punch.

A good, solid, almost professional blow to the chin.

Rich found it impossible to maintain a thought. For a few terrible seconds he lost track of where he was. Dreaming? Another blow jarred him. No, not dreaming. They always stop in my dreams. The attackers always walk away in my dreams.

The crowd was getting edgy, disgusted. Rich was just standing there, allowing himself to be beaten up. Scattered voices urged him, "Give a little back, man . . . Fight."

Are they really concerned with me, Rich wondered. Or are they bothered by the quality of today's show? Some wanted him to fight; others wanted him to flip. Rich knew there could be only one victory: He had to disappoint everyone. He couldn't fight without feeling sick, and he couldn't flip without feeling crazy. As it was, Rich's only reaction was that of his head whipping back from an especially strong blow.

Longhair backed off. "Is that all there is?" he demanded.

Rich said nothing.

Longhair dismissed him with a snort. "Always trying to change the world, aren't you? Sitting in the back of class smarting off with the answers all the time. Don't you ever do anything but read books, *boy*?"

Rich sniffed. His nose was beginning to trickle blood. He made no reply.

"You're not so smart after all, are you? I may not know what the capital of South America is, but I got a girlfriend and you don't. And I bet you think about that all the time, don't you?"

Rich said nothing. The blood tasted salty on his lips.

Longhair nodded. "You're not going to change the world today, are you, *boy*? *This* is the world. You getting beat up in an empty lot is the world. I'm a man and

13

you're a boy and that is the world. It don't change." Long-hair shook his head. "Even if it did, a wimp like you couldn't change it."

Longhair turned and merged with the crowd. He and his friends quickly disappeared. The spectators, quiet now, broke away from each other and headed either home or towards the buses.

Alone Rich sat down slowly on the gravel of the lot.

They came for the Rich McFadden flip-out, he thought. They came, and they left disappointed because they thought it didn't happen. It did happen, only they just didn't notice. The flip-out was all internal. The flip-out was no reaction at all.

When Rich was eight years old he had just two goals in life—to go to China and to get a dog. He tried to attain his first goal by sneaking out of the yard and wandering up and down the side streets of the neighborhood where they lived, on an Air Force base in Missouri. Rich never got lost in his search for China, but it upset his parents so much they tried to distract him by providing his second goal. They got him a dog, a big black terrier he named Winnie. Unfortunately, Winnie shared some of Rich's personality; he was always off somewhere, tearing into garbage cans, having a grand old time. Rich's father ranted and raved and finally had the dog put to sleep. Rich stopped leaving the yard without permission. He was afraid he would be put to sleep as well.

Sitting there in the lot, Rich picked at the tuft of grass near where his glasses lay. He lifted them, examining the lenses. Unbroken. The frames were bent, but he could repair them if he was careful. Mom didn't have to find out. He wiped the blood from his face with his palm, but not his sleeve. No blood on the clothes. Just an accident in gym class.

Rich was a distant, intelligent-looking boy with wide eyes, a narrow nose, and lips which, except when blood-ied, appeared so thin as to be nonexistent. He wore a turtleneck sweater under a sheepskin jacket, and jeans which were clean, if not exactly stylish. He sat, bruised and bloody but also brooding. *Why not*, he wondered.

14

Why not fight? This nightmare would end if he could just fight back.

Aching for the thought, Rich realized all of this would pass. If everyone who stood on this lot today, cheering, were to return to this lot in ten years time, would they want a bloody fight to root for? No. He was sure of that. They would be adults—calm, rational adults who would hate violence as much as he did now. Should he be ashamed for being the first to understand this?

Rich sighed, climbing to his feet. Maybe you couldn't change the world, but it didn't hurt to let the world know who you were. Just as soon as you found out yourself.

Three

Jenny stood with Marcie Price near the bleachers of the Travers Air Force Base track and football field. She and Marcie were trying to prevent Patty from stuffing herself beneath the bleachers. Patty clawed her way under the red-stained wood framework as several huffing and puffing figures in sweatsuits jogged past. "Oh, my God!" shrieked Patty. "Did he see me?"

"I think so," said Marcie. "He waved."

Patty rose up some, peeking out between two levels of bleachers. She was a straight-haired blonde with blue eyes that rarely focused on any one thing for too long. "Which guy?" she asked.

"Him." Marcie gestured.

Patty screamed, again ducking for cover. "Don't point!"

Jenny shook her head and watched the track and the runners. She felt nervesick. Her stomach was wrapped in a familiar knot; she was almost lightheaded with anticipation. Apprehension. Classic, she thought. First you lose time as if it were change slipping from a hole in your pocket, and now your entire body is falling apart. Only a matter of paperwork before you find yourself weaving baskets in some antiseptic home for The Kids Who Couldn't Make It.

Marcie made a sarcastic comment about Patty's cowardice and lifted the boom box again. Marcie's eyes were hidden behind square wire-rimmed glasses and fierce red hair that got tangled by the wind and covered much of her face. The boom box belonged to Patty, but Marcie lugged it about dutifully. The new *Walrus* tape was inside and Marcie kept rewinding and playing one song again and again. It was called "Once More Without Feeling."

"*Once more without the reasons . . .*
Let's have it once more without feeling."

Marcie shook her head as she pushed the buttons to rewind again. "I thought that was why we came down here. So you could see him."

"We did." Patty looked over from beneath the bleachers. "I just don't want him to see *me*."

"Where exactly did you meet this guy?" asked Jenny. She wondered if Patty actually had met him, or if this was another complicated Patricia Myer Fantasy Love Affair. Patty was able to generate all of the required emotions for a romantic relationship—infatuation, love, jealousy, hurt, heartbreak, hatred—all without ever having done more than exchange a passing "hello" with her alleged lover. The most recent example of this had been her torrid relationship with Mr. Ludwig, the biology teacher at school. Patty didn't even take biology.

"I met him at a squadron party."

"Which squadron?"

"Who knows? I only got to talk to him a few minutes before we had to go. His name is Brian. He said he was on the base varsity football team and I should come by and say hello."

"So go say hello."

"No!"

"Is he a capsule jock?" asked Marcie. A capsule jock was a missile launch officer, like Jenny's dad. A lot of the younger officers were capsule jocks.

"No." Patty shook her head. "I don't even think he's an officer."

"You're better off with an officer."

"I know. I don't care."

Jenny squinted, watching the players begin their workout. It was the wing varsity team all right, comprised of players from squadrons all over the base. For some reason Jenny was reminded of her fish as she watched them, and the thought amused her. The players darting about, in and out of groups, just like the red bettas. Jenny shook her head. "He doesn't look all that old. Probably just out of high school."

"How old do you think he is?" Patty asked. She sounded anxious.

Jenny changed the subject. "So what ever happened to Rick Waters?"

"What?"

"That guy whose dad just transferred in from Germany. Remember?" She mocked Patty, " 'Oh, Jenny, he speaks German and *everything.*' "

Marcie joined in, swooning, " 'Oh, he's so *beautiful.*' "

Patty shot them both dirty looks.

So Marcie answered the question and earned herself another dirty look from Patty. "She saw Rick at the movies with some girl last Friday, and she thinks he was cheating on her."

Patty sounded annoyed. "I thought you weren't going to say anything."

Marcie shrugged. "There are no secrets among the weird."

Patty looked up at Jenny. "The relationship was dying anyway. The passion was just too intense. We were both burning out."

Marcie laughed. "You never even talked to him."

"What we had together went way beyond words," said Patty. "I'll never forget him."

Marcie was still laughing. "I'm sure he'll hold you fondly in his heart as well."

"That all sounds so sharp coming from Miss Said No To Billy Brooks."

Jenny perked up. "What?" Billy Brooks was the vice-president of the Student Council, very cute, and very popular. Jenny had lost track of the number of girls dying to go out with him.

Patty said, "Billy Brooks asked Marcie to the Homecoming dance and she told him to space off."

"I was polite."

"Right. Tell her why you said no."

Marcie frowned. "I want to go with Dave Meely."

18

Patty shrieked again. "He is such a geek!"

"No, he isn't," said Marcie. "I sit next to him in natural sciences. He makes me laugh."

Terrific, thought Jenny, and she meant it sincerely. Finally a reason to go out with somebody other than the fact that he made the "A" Cute List. She shrugged, still watching the figures on the field and still thinking about her fish. Marcie had played through the song once more and was rewinding again.

"There he is!" Patty whispered now, diving from sight.

Jenny couldn't help frowning. Patty was beautiful and had twice as many friends as either she or Marcie did, but Patty was confident that any guy she might be interested in was sure to reject and humiliate her. It had been Patty's idea to come down to the football field, and now she was burrowed beneath the bleachers. Patty had declared it "absolutely essential" that they go watch football practice. Patty was always declaring something or other to be "absolutely essential." She had met another beautiful guy. Another beautiful guy she needed to go hide from.

Must be nice, Jenny thought. Then she shook her head. "Patty, this is crazy. What are you going to do when practice ends?"

Patty hesitated. "What do you think I should do?"

Marcie interrupted. "Why not tell him the truth?" She had stopped rewinding the tape and was letting it play through. "Tell him that you love him more than the breath of life itself, and would like to either have his baby or go to the movies. Whichever is more convenient."

"Marcie!"

They watched a few more minutes of practice. Guys were now tossing footballs and crashing into one another. Marcie asked, "What if this guy is like twenty-seven years old or something? Would your Dad let you go out with him?"

"Hardly."

"Then why are we here?"

"What Daddy doesn't know hasn't gotten me grounded yet."

"Ah, but does your dream guy know your dad is the Wing King?"

"It won't come up."

"No, I suppose it won't if you never talk to him."

Patty smirked. "Listen, we need a plan. What if he comes over here? Should we act like we just happened to be passing by?"

Marcie groaned. "Oh, come on . . ."

"We could say we're waiting for your brother."

Jenny smiled. "Tell him you just came by to gawk at his body."

"Hey!"

"I'll tell him," said Marcie. She waved a hand high over her head. "Hey, Brian!"

Patty screamed from beneath the bleachers but found she could not really burrow under any further. Jenny laughed because Marcie, as always, had no shame. As for the players, they did not seem to have even heard and were lining up again for a scrimmage.

Patty peeked out at Jenny. "So when are you and Kirk going to get back together?"

"We're not."

"Why?"

"I just don't feel that way about him."

"But he's so cute."

"Go for it. He's available."

Patty frowned. "You're always so cold. You're the poet. I always thought poets were hot-blooded and emotional. You're too calm, Jenny."

"Right." Jenny was watching the red bettas—the football players—dart about the tank—the field.

"I don't think I've ever seen you upset. About anything." Patty sounded almost confused. "Why is that?"

Why is that, thought Jenny. Because when I get upset, they call doctors.

"Jenny doesn't get upset," said Marcie. She had set the tape deck down on the grass.

"That's not right for a poet," Patty pronounced. "I read a poem once that said if you could not hurt then you could not love."

20

Jenny didn't respond.

"He's going to ask you to the dance."

"What?"

"Kirk. He's going to ask you to the Homecoming dance."

"How do you know?"

"He told me in art class today."

Definitely classic, thought Jenny. I have become a *topic*. A subject for conversations, an issue to be debated in art class in between requests to please pass the crayons.

"Are you going to go with him?"

"No."

"Who are you going with?"

"I don't think I'm going."

"This is your junior year Homecoming. You have to go."

"There are more vital issues in the world than whether or not I go to the Homecoming," Jenny said.

"Name one."

Marcie looked up. "Nuclear war."

Jenny and Patty both stared at her.

Marcie held up something she was reading. It was a mimeographed flyer of the type passed out on street corners and left in stacks near the front of supermarkets. Marcie read the flyer aloud, " 'Stop the Nightmare needs you . . .' "

"Let me see," Patty said.

Marcie handed it down.

"Where did you get that?" asked Jenny.

"Off base last night. I forgot I even had it. It was folded up in my jacket pocket."

Patty read it, then handed it back up to Jenny. Patty's attention had returned to the football practice, but she said, "Weird. I think that's from the same guy who was in class yesterday."

Jenny looked at the flyer. BEYOND THE NUCLEAR FREEZE—SAVE THE CHILDREN, it read. Another guilt trip, she thought. Another reason to lie awake at night.

"He's painting you," Patty said.

"What?" Jenny was losing track of the subject now.

21

"I swear. Kirk has your prom picture from last year and he's doing a portrait of you in oils from it. So far he's doing a real good job."

Jenny sighed now. Why couldn't things just go back to the way they had been before the summer, before she had started to go out with Kirk? Why couldn't he just become Kirk from school again? Why couldn't he just be somebody she said hello to in the mornings again? Instead, there was this huge blob out there, apparently thinking about her night and day. He still called, still stopped by the house, and now he was painting her in art class. But the worst part was the creepy idea of somebody lying out there at night *thinking about her.*

"He still loves you," said Patty.

"Yeah?" asked Jenny. "So what is love?"

"Love is when somebody paints you in oils."

"I don't think so."

"At least he cares," said Patty. "Who do you care about these days?"

"I'm in between caring."

"That sounds really wonderful."

Marcie jumped in, off the subject. "You know what poem of yours I really liked? That one about you and Kirk. What was it called?" Marcie was searching her memory, and since Jenny suspected there would be many drawers and closets in her mind to go through before she found the answer, she went ahead and supplied it.

" 'Why Me?' "

Marcie nodded quickly. "Yeah. 'Why me? Out of all the girls in the world, why me?' "

"Why did you and Kirk break up?" Patty asked.

Jenny shrugged. "He never answered the question."

Patty shook her head and looked back to the field.

Jenny felt really annoyed now. "Well, what about you? You're out here having this weird affair with a guy you won't even let see you. You'll never even go out with him."

"I might if he ever asks me."

"First he would have to hire a private detective to find you," Marcie cut in.

"The time isn't quite right yet. When it is, we will be with each other, and words will not be necessary."

Patty turned back to Jenny. She looked serious. "I think you and Kirk should get back together. I think it's absolutely essential. There is a void in your life now, and when there are too many voids in your life, you can become a void."

"Meaning?"

"Be careful."

"I'm always careful," said Jenny. Which was true.

"I just don't want you to forget to live. You work too hard at things. Like school. You have to learn to unwind."

"Tell me that after I win a scholarship."

"I just don't want you to mess up."

Jenny was suddenly very annoyed. "Who are you to judge my life?"

Patty paused. "I thought I was your friend."

Jenny closed her eyes. "Give it a rest, Patty."

Marcie stopped the conversation. The coach on the field was calling for a water break, and Marcie sarcastically said, "I think it's absolutely essential we forget everything else and concentrate on Ms. Patricia's problem."

Jenny looked at Marcie, who was smiling. Patty also turned. "Why? What's wrong?"

Marcie pointed. "Brian's on his way over here."

Patty screamed, Marcie laughed, and pretty soon after that, Jenny went home. She walked there directly but didn't hurry and arrived sometime between five and five-twenty. She wasn't really sure; she was losing track of spare minutes now. The idea worried her. What had happened to the time?

Was she really prepared to find out?

Jenny went quietly upstairs, hoping to avoid major difficulties, but she stopped in the open doorway of her room. There was no sign of her stepbrother around—at least his bedroom door was shut—but the Cockroach Woman was home. She was sitting on Jenny's rumpled bed, reading from a stack of papers. Even from the hall Jenny recognized the page she was reading. It was her most recent suicide note, written just the day before. In her goodbye to the world, Jenny had tried to start a poem:

He stood his ground until an army came,
and ground him where he stood.

Standing in the doorway, Jenny watched but didn't move. Couldn't move. She felt consumed by hopelessness. She remembered the terrible scene after school that day. A boy from her English class had been beaten up badly. It was violence. Not the casual plastic gunfire of television, but a terrible reality. Someone who was real, someone she knew was real, was left bloody for no good reason.

Jenny had felt fear, but not for the boy. For herself. She had stood with a crowd that was becoming of one mind. A crowd beast, like in the old Roman Empire movies where the audience cheered as men hacked each other to pieces. He never raised a hand to protect himself, and that was the real horror of it to the animal crowd. Not the terrible beating, but the fact that he accepted it without struggling. They saw it as pathetic. They saw it as wrong.

Jenny disagreed. Although she claimed no real knowledge of the subject, she had read about Karma and the forces that were said to bind the universe. Watching the beating, she wondered if the boy was trying to inflict spiritual retaliation against his attacker. He was cut, his nose was bleeding, but the long-haired punk doing it to him seemed spooked. Jenny wondered if his soul was being battered with every punch he threw.

The Cockroach Woman noticed her now, and she almost spat the words. "So are you crazy again? Is that it?"

Jenny cringed, stepping back into the hall. She felt another chill. The Cockroach Woman was a creature with no regard for personal privacy. She stood up, laying the papers aside on the bed. "I guess I was wrong about you not needing to see a doctor anymore. Do you really want to die?"

Jenny moved into the doorway and leaned against the frame.

"Answer me!"

"I don't know."

"You don't know?" The Cockroach Woman almost shrieked it. She was shaking her head. "What do I do that is so bad?"

Jenny didn't know what to say, so she looked at the Hairy Werewolf. The Hairy Werewolf clock was a gift from Wesley who, at twelve, could not be expected to know any better. It was five-forty-three p.m.

"Do I ask you to call me Mom? No. But do you call me Amy, like a reasonable person? Also no." She lifted a fistful of papers. "Is this what you call me around your friends? The Cockroach Woman?"

Jenny said nothing. She set her handbag on the dresser and caught Amy Polson's reflection in the mirror as she paced the room. Like a vampire, the Cockroach Woman shed no image of her own. She was always reflected as Amy Polson Westphal. She was passing before the empty aquarium now.

Empty.

"The fish!" Jenny ran to the tank. "What happened to my fish?" The filter pump and heater had been disconnected and the water drained. It had been done quickly; the filter pump still leaked droplets, and a few scattered bits of colored gravel littered the wet tank bottom.

The Cockroach Woman spoke between clenched teeth. "Since you seem so prone to self-destruction, I decided to get rid of the fish now and save trouble later."

Jenny lost a breath and said very coldly, "You are sick."

Crack! The Cockroach Woman—Amy Polson?—slapped Jenny hard across the face. Jenny straightened herself, cheek burning red, but refused to raise a hand to it.

"Aren't you going to cry? I thought you cried all the time."

Jenny breathed, counting time. Button down. The small voice was there again. Button down.

The next was frightening. The Cockroach Woman suddenly became Amy Polson Westphal as Jenny watched. Amy Polson Westphal shivered, and strength faded from

25

her eyes. Her voice broke. "I . . . I'm sorry. I didn't mean to hit you. I shouldn't, I . . ."

She recovered some. "These notes scare me, Jenny. Why are you writing them? Why are you hiding them up here?"

"They weren't hidden too well, were they?"

Jenny immediately regretted saying it.

Too late. Amy Polson drew tall. For a moment it was hard to tell who she was, or who she wanted to be. Then the Cockroach Woman spoke. "You need help."

"I need to be left alone."

"Look, Jenny, I really don't know how much more of this I can stand. You treat me lousy, you treat Wesley lousy—"

"I do not treat Wesley bad!"

"Yes, you do!" Now Amy Polson was yelling, and there was a trace of the stammer. Jenny would have considered the yelling a minor victory if she hadn't felt bad about the stammer. Amy Polson had a slight speech impediment; she stuttered when upset or nervous.

"Look." She struggled to get it out. "I'm sorry. I don't understand why you hate me so much."

"I don't hate you. I just don't need you."

"Right." Amy Polson nodded. "Who do you need, Jenny?"

Strange question. "I don't know," Jenny said.

"Well, well. Isn't it wonderful having all the answers?"

Jenny just looked at her.

Amy Polson seemed to find calm. "I know that you're upset. I realize your mother's birthday is coming up . . ."

Jenny tried to block it out. "Shut up."

"And I know I'll never be your mother . . ."

Jenny felt herself shaking. "Leave my mother out of this."

Amy Polson rattled on. "She's gone, Jenny. You need to accept that."

"I don't need anything, except to see her."

"See her?" The Cockroach Woman reared herself. "Your mother is dead, Jenny."

Jenny didn't react. Not outwardly. "Just because she

26

doesn't want to see me right now doesn't mean that she's dead."

"You know she's dead, Jenny."

"I know she's alive."

"How many times . . . ?"

"You know what I think? I think you're all crazy. And I think the only reason you want me to think she's dead is so I won't know you're hiding me from her. She and Captain Daddy never got along. Everybody knew that."

"Okay." The Cockroach Woman tried another approach. "Why doesn't she answer your letters?"

"She's very busy."

"Then why don't you call her?"

"What?"

"Call her," said the Cockroach Woman. "Pick up the phone and call her. Do it now."

Jenny shivered. "Leave my mother out of this. Shut up about her. Okay? Whatever else you want, okay. Fine. Wonderful." Jenny didn't know what else to add.

The Cockroach Woman started to leave the room but paused when she noticed something on the floor by the dresser. It was the mimeographed flyer which Marcie had given to Patty, and Patty had passed to her. Jenny wasn't sure why it was here; she didn't remember keeping it. The Cockroach Woman snatched it up. "What's this?"

Jenny sighed, desperate for a chance to button down. "Just an announcement for some meeting."

The Cockroach Woman read it with no change of expression. She crumpled the paper into a ball and dropped it into the trash basket. "Crap."

Jenny watched her go. She wondered if Amy Polson was really a cruel and inconsiderate person, or whether these things were just accidents. Slips, maybe. Jenny hated herself for caring about what the Cockroach Woman thought.

In fact, Jenny didn't feel she even knew herself. Was it possible to hate someone you didn't know? Then again, was it even possible to know yourself? That was probably just a lot of Hollywood garbage designed for people who

27

went off on cross-country treks or off to war to "find themselves."

So what happens now?

Jenny gathered the papers from the floor and the bed. Amy Polson had obviously come across the shoebox at the bottom of the closet and thought it contained love letters or other mushy stuff. Jenny could picture her excitedly carrying the box to the bed and beginning to read. Then came the shock. Jenny wondered if Amy Polson had really been frightened, or even more excited at the prospect of reading a suicide note. A stack of suicide notes.

Jenny smirked. Who was the sick one in this bunch?

She didn't tear the notes up. Why bother? Instead she stuffed them back into the box and returned them to the closet. Evidence against herself maybe, but she had to keep them. Some people made sudden decisions to end their lives. They came home from a bad day and decided to open their wrists in the bathtub. They hung themselves while changing clothes. Or ate everything in the medicine cabinet as a midnight snack. Opportunity knocked, and they answered, but they left everyone around them wondering why. Sometimes, as an afterthought, the soon to be departed would take the time to scribble some vague, often cryptic note which usually only added to the mystery.

If and when I make the trip, Jenny had decided, I will be leaving volumes. There may be questions, but nobody will ever ask why.

She shut the closet and thought about it. If you were really going to look for yourself, couldn't you make the search without leaving your own room? Or was wandering around in your own mind the fastest of all possible ways to go crazy?

Jenny trembled with a force that scared her and made her lay back on the bed until it passed. Before, when she used to cry over everything, she spent most of her time quiet, alone, and thinking. Wandering around in her own mind.

Had she been crazy? For real?

Jenny waited until her limbs were sufficiently calm and

her stomach cranked back to medium turmoil, then she stood. Wherever I may find myself, it will not be in this room. I am not in the closet, tucked away in a drawer, or stashed beneath a pillow.

She pulled the mimeographed flyer from the trash basket and read it again, trying to smile.

Opportunity knocked for those who could hear the sound over the beating of their own heart.

Four

"I've got an appointment for you to see the Air Force recruiter on Monday."

Rich looked up from his dinner, across the hardwood table to his father. Gus McFadden was slowly chewing on meatloaf.

"You did what?"

Gus McFadden stopped chewing. "I'm not trying to force you into anything. You've got a whole year left to make up your mind. I just want you to consider all of your options."

"What about college?"

Gus smiled. "What? Do you want to be an officer?"

Rich shook his head. "I don't want to go into the service at all."

Gus continued eating, but he said, "Don't go knocking what it is that puts bread in your mouth."

Rich just stared at his father for a minute. Gus was a heavyset man with a thick shadow of whiskers across his face. Despite a dedicated shave every morning, by mid-afternoon Gus was wearing a shadow again. "I don't want to enlist," Rich finally said.

Gus lumped some mashed potatoes together and spooned them up. "It's not like you have anything else going."

"So where am I supposed to be going?"

Gus looked up. "What?"

Rich shook his head. "It's not important."

Gus snorted. "Probably not." He went back to eating.

Rich watched him eat—consume was a better word—and wondered how these conversations started. How did these ideas pop into Gus's head? What was he supposed to do? Cure cancer to prove that he wanted to be a doctor? How was he supposed to explain?

His mother reentered the dining room. Ellen McFadden was a frail, fragile woman with blond hair and large wide eyes that startled easily. She settled behind a salad bowl and started to eat slowly, nibbling. She was on yet another diet.

Rich's brother, Mike, who had said nothing during the bickering, asked now to be excused. He silently shook his head at Rich. What was that? Sympathy? Contempt?

"Where are you going?" asked Gus.

"Dad . . ."

"Tell me or stay in the seat."

"I'm going over to Tracy's, okay?"

"Tracy? She new?"

"Dad . . ."

Gus smirked. "You stay out of trouble."

"I live for trouble."

"I know that."

Mike disappeared. Gus turned to Rich now. "You going to the football game tomorrow night?"

"No."

"So why not?"

"I don't like football."

"You don't support your school?"

"I hate my school."

"You're supposed to be true to your school."

"That's just a song, Dad."

Gus nodded. "There'll probably be a lot of girls there."

"There are a lot of girls in Australia, but you never offered me an airline ticket there."

Gus snarled a bit. "Don't be smart." He returned to his dinner. Four years earlier, Gus McFadden had had his photograph published in the base paper, the Travers *Traveller*. SHARP MISSILE SERGEANT TAKES FIVE SAC AWARDS. Rich always thought of his dad like that, as he had appeared in the yellowing newspaper clipping

31

tucked away upstairs. His face smug and proud. Only the headline was always different. SHARP MISSILE SERGEANT CALLS ELDEST SON AN IDIOT, or SHARP MISSILE SERGEANT EMBARRASSED AGAIN BY GEEK SON, and now SHARP MISSILE SERGEANT HAS FATHERED A BOY WHO DOESN'T LIKE TO PLAY OR WATCH FOOTBALL.

Rich didn't feel hungry anymore. He hadn't really felt hungry in the first place, but he continued to play with his food. Gus was still digging away. He was talking to his wife about the upcoming SAC Inspector General inspection of the base, the wing, and the Minuteman missile systems. "The IG" it was called. A surprise inspection, but everyone could guess within a few weeks of when it would hit. The team hit Travers Air Force Base once every eighteen months.

"Could be a recall in the morning," he was saying as he ate. "IG team could be here any time."

"Will you be pulling double shifts?"

"At least. I might wind up in the missile field for a few days. I better start keeping a bag packed."

She nodded.

Gus dropped his fork onto his plate and pushed it away. Rich's mother snatched it up immediately and vanished into the kitchen. The model dominated wife, Rich thought. Gus took the time to light up a menthol cigarette, then looked at Rich. "So what is it exactly that you want to do with your life?"

Rich shrugged. Not an easy pop question. He answered, "I'm not sure. Who can be sure? I just want it to have some meaning."

Gus flipped some ashes away. "There is no meaning in the world. You'll go a lot further if you stop trying to fix things all the time and learn to adjust."

"So what's wrong with trying to change the world?"

"It's not easily done."

"Nobody ever said it had to be easy."

Rich's mother returned then from the kitchen. She had cleared away most of the dishes and now lit up her own smoke. Again, Rich grimaced. He had tried to convince them both to quit for health reasons. His mother had smiled, still smoking. His father had ordered him to mind his own business.

"So what if it isn't your place to change the world?" Gus said.

"What if it is? What would you say if I wanted to be a doctor?"

"You? A doctor?"

Wonderful reaction, thought Rich. So supportive. His mother appreciated the thought, though. She said, "I think that's a wonderful idea. A doctor in the family."

Gus seemed to be mulling it over. "Do you know how much a medical officer makes?"

Rich got disgusted then, and it blurted out. "Why does absolutely everything have to be Air Force with you? There is a real world out there. With people, and civilian things, and friends you don't lose every few years."

Gus nodded. He stubbed his smoke out in the ash tray. "Yeah, there's a real world out there. But it's cold, real cold. And it doesn't care about you."

Right, thought Rich. So what's the difference?

He stood up to take his plate into the kitchen, but his father stopped him before he could move. "Rich, our family has been a service family for six generations. All the way back to the Civil War."

Rich nodded. He had heard the story before.

"The McFaddens had barely got off the boat before the shooting started then. It wasn't even their country. But there was a job to be done, and they did it. That's the kind of world it was. To survive, they fought. That's the kind of world it is. To survive, you fight."

"People don't always have to hurt each other . . ."

"Sometimes you do."

Rich took a breath.

Gus was still rambling. "I know you think we're strange, we're different. Well, you're right. We are. Military families like us are never really part of the community. I hardly ever bother to vote. Military families are like Gypsies. We come and go, come and go. Almost citizens, but

33

not quite. But it is special. That's all I'm trying to say. We hang together, and we take care of our own."

Rich nodded. Yeah, like a pack of wolves that hunt together. But he couldn't say that. He took his plate into the kitchen and scraped what was left of his dinner into the garbage disposal, stacking it on top of the small pile beside the sink.

Weird, weird discussions. And the topic was always Rich, it seemed. Gus always wanted to know why Rich didn't have a girlfriend yet, a "sweetheart" he called her. Rich hesitated in the kitchen. He didn't feel like rejoining the "Let's All Figure Out How To Help Rich" roundtable.

Things always got especially strange when the topic was "Rich and his future." Everything got so out of hand. Ambition? Goals? Well, all right.

It was wise and fine to have ambition and goals, just make sure they're readily understandable. Something that could be laid flat across the dinner table and quickly grasped.

My ambition?

I want to be a truck driver. Okay, great. Roll on.

My goal?

I want to be a fireman. Fantastic. Eat some smoke for me, son.

If you wanted to be a doctor because medics made wheelbarrows full of money, that was something they could easily understand. Say that you wanted to help others, and they worried. Say that you wanted to devote your life to maybe making the world a better place to live, and they called for a quiet consultation with the little men in the clean white jackets.

Rich shrugged. Life goes on, whether you can deal with it properly or not. So just duck low and aim yourself forward. Something was bound to work out, right? Rich pushed out of the kitchen and passed through the dining room. Everyone else had cleared out. He grabbed the paperback book he had been reading before dinner and hurried upstairs, still bothered.

Medicine. Yeah, maybe that was the way to go. The idea had been gnawing at Rich more and more. His grades were respectable enough, he knew. There might even be a scholarship in the works. College should be no problem. Could he see himself as a pre-med student?

Maybe.

Rich reached his bedroom door, which was directly across a small hall from his brother's room, and he checked the tape seal he carefully placed at the bottom of his door each morning, or whenever he had to step out for a while. Unbroken. It usually was, but he was paranoid and couldn't be sure. He peeled the tape back and went inside, bracing himself for the brown.

Rich's bedroom wore a bizarre shade of brown, one that sapped the very strength from him. He had yet to manage repainting it. Instead, he kept himself insulated in books, magazines, and every other conceivable sort of reading material. Rich read everything he saw, from soup labels to the front pages of newspapers in locked racks. He read the washing instructions sewn into his shirt collars and the words scrawled on sidewalks. He read encyclopedia articles and dictionary definitions.

A doctor? Get real, kid.

Rich collapsed back onto his bed. Why not? He tossed the paperback aside, thinking about it. Often, in study hall at school, Rich would sit plotting. On sheets of closely lined notebook paper he would address the ills of the world. The economy a mess? Zap the wealthy, absolutely no mercy. Go to the wall with the conglomerates. Pollution? Make the waste producers liable. Two dollars for each dollar's worth of devastation. But every time Rich thought himself close to a breakthrough, he would look up to discover some girl in study hall staring at him.

That would mean the end of all rational thought.

But medicine as a career?

Rich remembered his confrontation with the guidance counselor at the beginning of the school year. Like every other junior he had been scheduled to take the tests and see Mr. Crouse. Mr. Crouse had asked him about his immediate goals following high school. "The Peace Corps," Rich had replied.

"The Peace Corps?" Mr. Crouse nodded, pretending to be impressed. "Fantastic. But why?"

"I want to make a difference."

Mr. Crouse nodded again. Rich knew what he was thinking. Another loser. The public servant with yet another excuse to avoid getting a real job. But had Rich yet considered the possible benefits of an engineering degree?

Rich took a moment to prepare himself for all the endless arguments he had anticipated with Gus over the matter. Become an engineer and you get caught in the grind. Every day at the office. Grind. Another worry about money. Grind. Bills, responsibilities. Grind.

Besides, you always heard stories of Peace Corps workers finding their true love hunched over a sand pit in Tunisia.

Me? A doctor? It was an idea.

If only he could prevent the thugs at school from finding out.

"Hey."

Rich looked up. Mike leaned in the doorway. He was wearing a hat, which was strange. "Hey, what?" Rich responded.

"Can I borrow your denim jacket?"

"I don't know."

"Why don't you know?"

"I don't know if I appreciate the thought of my clothes having a better time than I am."

"Don't be stupid," said Mike. "I don't feel sorry for you."

"No?" Rich sat up.

"No. I know all about you. Girls? All you gotta do is ask."

"I can't tolerate rejection."

"You get used to it."

"Even you?"

Mike laughed. "Especially me. To go out with ten girls you have to ask fifty."

Rich nodded. "Free advice . . ."

" . . . is worth exactly what you pay for it," Mike finished. They laughed. It was an old line of Gus's.

"Take the jacket," Rich said. Then he asked, "Why are you wearing that hat?"

"I don't want to be recognized."

"Why?"

"I've got a bad reputation around Cheryl's house."

"I thought you were going to Tracy's."

"I lied."

Rich smirked. "Get out of here."

"I'm gone!" said Mike, grabbing the jacket from the pile on the closet floor. He hesitated in the doorway, though, not quite leaving. He put the jacket on and said, "You know what I want to see some day?"

"I couldn't begin to make a list . . . ," Rich responded.

"I want to see you just haul off and smack the daylights out of one of those thugs after school. Especially that long-haired creep. You could, you know."

"Yeah. But then what?"

"Then it would be over. They wouldn't bother you anymore."

"A lot of things bother me," said Rich. "I wish I could smack the daylights out of everything that bothers me, but what would happen then?"

Mike shrugged and disappeared.

Rich leaned back over the edge of the bed now. His journal, *Lonerman's Notebook*, stared him in the face, but he pushed it aside. On the front cover was an inscription, pressed on with a ballpoint pen: "It's Easier On The Soul To Suffer An Indignity Than To Inflict One."

Was that still true?

When Rich lifted his head again, his mother was standing in the open doorway. Smiling. Sort of.

Rich gave a wave. "Hey."

He waited for the reaction.

He expected some yelping—valid yelping—about the condition of his room, but instead her smile faded a bit and she asked, "Any problems at school today?"

Rich wondered if it was written on his face. The pain was in his stomach again. Yes, he thought. Something happened at school today, but it was just the usual nightmare and nothing I plan on talking about. I'm still trying

37

to bury the horrors in their own individual holes somewhere.

Relieve the day . . .

Standing in the hall, wildly spinning the combination on his dinged locker. The word GEEK! had been painted there long before, but he no longer noticed it. Not really. Until the girl from his English class walked by. The girl was very pretty, which meant that she was very scary. Rich made a special effort not to look up as she walked by, but as she did, she smiled and said, "Hi!"

What did that mean?

Given the unfair judgment of the universe according to Rich McFadden, he felt it a valid question. One that had to be asked. Because he had felt the chill before, the sick feeling that came whenever he started deluding himself that maybe somebody out there liked him. It always went badly.

Rich felt frustrated, annoyed with all the guys who treated girls casually, who talked to them all the time. It made him crazy. Football players. The popular ones. The guys who got the leads in the school plays and walked the halls on Valentine's Day carrying four or five carnations.

All of this was followed by the nightmare of world history class. A very different sort of girl, Lisa Collins, sat at the desk immediately in front of Rich, and she had spent the morning torturing him again.

He guessed she got a giggle from it. Mr. Pollack had called another free study period so he could read his magazines, and that meant you could talk so long as you didn't get loud. Lisa twisted around at her desk, bored, and she began to interrogate Rich. She was a thin-faced girl with vacant eyes and twisted, streaked blond hair. She asked, "Are you going to the Homecoming dance?"

Trying not to shudder, Rich said nothing. She already knew the answer to that one.

"Why don't you ask Pam?" Lisa chimed. "Pam might go with you."

Pamela Voriss was a cheerleader, exceptionally pretty, and one of the most popular girls in school. Her father

38

was also a civilian, which was unusual. She was seated two rows over, chatting with Brad Ziegel, whose father was the commander of the security police squadron.

"I'll ask her for you," said Lisa. Before Rich could say anything, she called, "Hey, Pam!"

Pamela looked up. Brad looked up. Almost everybody in class looked up, with the exception of Mr. Pollack.

"Do you want to go to the Homecoming dance with Rich McFadden?"

Pamela made a face indicating what she thought of the idea and then turned back to Brad.

Rich shuddered again. When I die, he thought, it will be anticlimatic. I've died too many times before.

Lisa made a mocking frown and said, "Oh, wait a minute. I know. What about Laurie?"

Laurie Woodward was overweight, cruelly afflicted by acne, and almost as unpopular as Rich. She sat three seats over, scribbling in a notebook and pretending not to be embarrassed.

"Hey, Laurie!" Lisa called out. "Do you want to go to the dance with Rich?"

Laurie hunched over her desk.

"No way, huh?" Lisa asked. "Why not? You're not going to do any better, are you?"

Laurie pulled herself lower, closer to the paper. But it wasn't hard to see that she was crying.

"Come on, Laurie, you'll have a grand old time—"

"Why don't you just leave her alone?"

Lisa's eyes widened. Rich was surprised at himself for speaking, but Lisa was making Laurie Woodward cry, and that was absolutely nuts. Why bring her into this nightmare?

Rich repeated, "Why don't you just leave her alone? You want to bother me every day? Fine, enjoy. I'm easy. But leave her out of this."

Lisa sat back, shocked. She looked around, but everyone else had looked away. Finally Lisa turned back around in her seat. But Lisa was going with Lloyd Keller, and Lloyd Keller was nicknamed Longhair. So after school there had been Longhair to deal with.

39

And Rich had never raised a finger to defend himself. How can you expect to change the world if you can't even change yourself?

He looked up at his mom and said, "No, nothing much happened at school."

Almost a medical student, he thought. We have to be above all of that.

Mom sighed, leaning into the doorway. "What do you really want to do tomorrow night?" she asked.

Rich was confused. "What?"

"Do you have something planned? Instead of the football game?"

Rich shrugged. "Not really."

"I don't want you to feel forced into things. Decide for yourself what you want to do." She fumbled in a pocket and came out with a crumpled five dollar bill. "You could go to the movies. Or you could go down to the Mall bookstore and look around. You like that."

Rich nodded. "I might." For some reason his throat felt tight, his face hot.

Mom stood there another minute. Then she turned, and as she turned, she said, "Rich, I think you'd be a good doctor."

Then she was gone.

Suddenly Rich felt more depressed than ever. What did girls matter when you couldn't even survive yourself? He knew he couldn't sit around the house, even if it was a school night. Then he remembered the last event of the day. The flyer he had found on the way home from school.

Today was Thursday. The fourteenth of November.

The Stop the Nightmare meeting was scheduled for that evening in the Civic Center. He could attend, take part, maybe even make a small difference in how things went.

Yeah.

It was crazy. And dangerous. But he could go. He could take a stand. How different would that be? Not to flip out, but to take a stand and still not have to hurt anyone.

Rich grabbed his sheepskin jacket and left through the back door.

Five

The Civic Center was the brightest building on the block. On the street across from its high cement steps someone had mounted a red and white placard announcing the meeting. A few people still huddled outside, awaiting companions, and a photographer from the Greylake *News-Dispatch* ducked about snapping pictures. Jenny didn't loiter with the other stragglers. Stepping down from her bus, she paused at the street corner, then hurried up the steps.

Jenny had been to the Civic Center only once, when she was required to attend a City Council meeting for her social studies class the year before. She remembered the building as empty sounding, a place of hollow halls and a large vacant-looking auditorium. The entire City Council meeting had amounted to seven men and one woman sitting around a long oak table and being watched by fifteen spectators and two dozen empty folding chairs.

Tonight was different. The hard marble halls of the Center were softened by hand-lettered signs marking the way. Dark-eyed children cried down from posters, asking, WILL THERE BE A WORLD FOR US? The hall still echoed every footfall, but it was now populated with college student types talking among themselves and a mother tucked into a corner disciplining her excited young son. Burly men pressed their way into the auditorium—local ranchers, she guessed—and she wondered what they were doing there.

Edging down the hall, Jenny worried that she was suffering from brain bubbles. She had left the house to find herself, but was by now fairly certain that she was looking in the wrong place.

Who are you kidding? You didn't come here to find yourself. You came here to find Maxwell Neuger. Jenny shrugged. Just because you couldn't find yourself didn't mean that you had to go home empty-handed.

So what do you intend to go home with?

No answer.

So what is it? Are you in love? Are you hopelessly over the edge? Jenny didn't think so. Not love. Not even infatuation. She just wanted another look into his eyes.

Sounds like a Patty Myer style romance to me, she thought.

Five or six people were milling about, collecting names for a mailing list. Jenny frowned. Activist types. One man had the beginnings of a goatee beard, and a woman clung to him. Despite the weather she wore a peasant blouse, and her graying hair was tied back in a ponytail. They were trying to convince a teenage boy to add his name to an attendance list. The boy was doing his best to decline.

Feedback whined from the stage up front and was adjusted a few times before it stopped.

The teenage boy across from Jenny turned, meeting her eyes for just a moment. She recognized him in the same way she would have recognized her mother standing there. Hesitantly. Fearful. Something that had to be dealt with.

It was the boy from her English class. The one she had seen beaten up after school.

Seeing him there made Jenny think again about Karma and the circles that bound the universe together. What goes around, comes around. A few hours earlier she was thinking about him, and there he was. Looking at her. Jenny decided that, yes, this was something that had to be dealt with.

She stepped up beside him. "So, hi."

He jumped. He also seemed a little empty inside. Jenny recognized the look: It was the face she saw in the mirror. "Hello," he nodded.

42

"You're in my English class. Mrs. Adams?"

He paled, smiled weakly. "Yeah. Hi."

"I'm Jenny. Jenny Westphal."

"I know."

Jenny had to raise her eyebrows in question to get him to admit he was Rich McFadden.

Classic, Jenny thought. Two of us, both military dependents, both here against all reason, bound together by Karma, and we're both mental rejects. Misfits.

"I thought I was going to be the only one crazy enough to come down here," Rich said.

Jenny resisted the impulse to tell him that he was. After all, she was only an observer. She couldn't say that. Instead she smiled and said, "I was curious. That's all."

"I think everybody is. But not everybody came."

Jenny nodded. Then she said, "Hey, don't get the wrong idea or anything, but I needed to talk to you."

"You needed to talk to *me*?"

Jenny shrugged. How did you explain Karma and the binding of the universe to a guy based on the fact that you saw him beat up in a schoolyard? She shrugged. "Yeah. I don't know why. Your dad is Air Force too; I guess that's why. We're both taking the same chance."

"What chance is that?" Rich asked.

"Getting our rear ends thrashed."

The crowd was settling. Jenny sorted faces, listening intensely, but she couldn't find Maxwell Neuger. She said to Rich, "Maybe we better sit down."

He looked shocked, but agreed. "Do you want some punch or anything first?"

Jenny looked at the refreshment table, but her nerve-sickness was back; her stomach was in disarray. She shook her head. So they went and sat down. Rich looked around a lot. Suddenly he said, "Oh, here," and thrust a colorful pamphlet into Jenny's hands. It was entitled, BEYOND THE NUCLEAR FREEZE. "They're handing them out at the door," he explained.

Jenny flipped through the pamphlet. Then she looked at Rich. The wounds from the fight were still there; his

43

lower lip was caked with a crust of dried blood. Jenny didn't ask about it.

After a few minutes the conversations died down, and Reverend Mark Lowell stepped to the podium. He was in his mid-forties, wore a beard, and was in the newspapers frequently. "Sorry about the late start," he said. "I'm a bit out of practice. The last time I did this sort of thing was in 1970, at Berkleley."

There were some chuckles at that, and Reverend Lowell continued. "I hate to say it, but in a lot of ways I think our problems then were easier. The war wasn't something anyone could ignore. We looked it in the face every day. Our teenage boys were leaving us to fight it. Some were coming back blinded, maimed, crippled. Some weren't coming back at all. Every day we sat down to our dinners with the war right in front of us on the six o'clock news. We had war in technicolor. Body counts with our breakfast. Napalm was a household word."

Reverend Lowell shook his head as if to clear the image, raising his hands to emphasize the point. "The issue today is more difficult to get across because it's much more terrifying to everyone. Nobody wants to know that he could die. Nobody wants to look this issue in the face over breakfast. It's easier to turn away and hope that someone else will do something about it."

Reverend Lowell paused. "What we need is something more than just words on the subject. Passive resistance. Demonstrations. Non-violent action to draw attention to the cause, to remind the world that there are nuclear weapons right here in Greylake."

He smiled. "Now, I happen to think the next speaker is the last word on peaceful resistance. He brought himself out all the way from Lansing, Michigan to help us out. Allow me to present to you Mr. Maxwell Neuger . . ."

Jenny sat up with a jerk. Polite applause, led by Reverend Lowell, resounded through the auditorium as Maxwell Neuger appeared out of nowwhere and stepped up to the podium. Where had he been hiding himself? Jenny almost shivered. Her stomach did a small roll as she saw Neuger shake hands with Reverend Lowell. Neuger stood tall in tan slacks and a sport coat. Maxwell Neuger with his worried voice and his irregular face. Jenny could see the glint in his eyes. She watched him as he thanked Reverend Lowell and turned to face the audience.

He adjusted the microphone a bit. "I want to thank you all for coming out to see us tonight. I want to thank you for coming to hear what we have to say. I know in some instances that has taken a lot of courage. This is a military town, and some of your jobs are on the line here. Thank you again."

He launched into a variation of the "twenty-six minutes" speech that he had made in Jenny's sociology class, but Jenny lost track of his exact words. She was more concerned with his motives than his message. She wanted to know what drove him to be the *messenger*. She watched him closely as he spoke. He pleaded for peace, he pleaded for sanity. He said it was a common cause, but Jenny watched him very closely because she knew that somewhere behind his eyes was the real reason *why*.

Neuger concluded his speech by making an appeal for Stop the Nightmare. "We're opening a storefront office on Eighth Street. We'll be there for as long as the donations hold out. We think it's essential to get this message across and to continue getting this message across. We need your help, and I don't just mean your money. We need volunteers to help us out at the office, but most of all we just need you, all of you, and all of your friends. We need you to be there when we demonstrate against the base and against the presence of nuclear weapons within this state."

Neuger looked flushed, almost weak. "Remember the twenty-six minutes." He stepped back from the podium, and the applause swelled until Reverend Lowell replaced him at the podium and started relating the story of how he had spent Christmas Eve 1968 in a Bakersfield, California jail. Jenny tuned him out as she watched Neuger make his way out of the auditorium.

Without thinking about it she stood up. Pushing past Rich, she stumbled towards the aisle. She hurried past the reception table and out into the hall.

Empty.

Jenny walked down to the end of the hall. Every click of her heels echoed above the muffled words of Reverend Lowell. She stopped at the corner and looked left as casually as possible.

Empty again. Midway down this hall the lights had been left off. Jenny started to turn back when she heard the sound. A cough. She looked again down the hall, squinting towards the dark. A figure was leaning back against the wall, near a water fountain.

Slowly, Jenny started down. She stopped fifteen feet away. He had not even noticed her yet, or at least he wasn't bothering to look up. His eyes appeared closed, and he was still draped in shadows, but Jenny knew it was Neuger. Not Neuger shouting at a classroom or appealing to an auditorium, but Neuger tired and leaning back against a wall for support. Neuger alone, and probably wishing to remain that way.

Well, you've seen him, she thought. You've had your Patty Myer style fun for today. Is it time to go home yet?

She startled herself by speaking and startled herself even more by noticing that she was no longer nervesick. She felt calm. Buttoned down. "Hello?" she asked.

He opened his eyes. It took a moment, but he said, surprised perhaps, "Hello back."

"I want to help you."

He smiled but didn't say anything. "My name's Jenny Westphal. You talked to my sociology class. Mr. Bradley."

"You're from the base?"

Jenny nodded.

"And you want to help Stop the Nightmare?"

"I want to help you."

"Why?"

In that instant Jenny felt nervesickness fall on her like a wave, and she twisted on her heels, starting back up the hall.

"Wait."

The footsteps were behind her now, and Jenny stopped. Maxwell Neuger walked up beside her. "I'm sorry. I didn't mean it to sound that way."

46

"How did you mean it to sound?"

He frowned. "I guess I'm not feeling so terrific tonight. I think I'm getting one of your Montana colds."

Jenny stared at him. "Not mine. I'm from Indiana."

He smiled. "Then you know what I mean. I'm from Michigan."

"I know."

"I guess everybody does. I'm the nut from Michigan."

Jenny still felt sick, but she managed to return his smile. Up close now, Neuger's eyes looked tired and confused, not at all like the hypnotic personality she had seen in the classroom. Then again, he did look a bit sick and pale under the hall lights.

He held his smile. "If you still want to help us out, though, stop by the Eighth Street storefront any afternoon."

"I go to school," Jenny said.

Neuger shrugged. "Whenever you're free. We always need help."

Jenny nodded. "Okay."

Neuger grimaced slightly and then worked up another smile. "Thanks."

Jenny hesitated. "Are you okay?"

"Oh, yeah, I'm fine. Always fine. I think I ate too many of those excellent cookies inside." He started to excuse himself. "High level conference afterwards, you know. We have to decide what to do with all of the leftover punch."

Jenny watched him go and listened to his fading footsteps. She closed her eyes and tried communicating again. Are you there, friend? I suspect that I am very much in over my head now.

Returning to her seat, she sat next to Rich. He never even gave her a glance. At about ten-thirty the meeting started to break up.

Jenny followed Rich outside. On the cool steps of the Civic Center he paused to button his jacket. "Are you going to wait for the bus?" she asked.

Rich shook his head.

Jenny frowned at that. "What? Are you walking back?"

47

"Yeah."

"But it's ten miles."

"Only about five."

"Why are you doing it? Don't you have any money?"

"I'm doing it because I have all night."

Jenny didn't understand, but she didn't like to press. She stood there, waiting for Rich to leave. He took one step and then looked back. "Where do you know me from?" he asked.

Jenny blinked. "English class."

Rich waited.

Jenny swallowed. She tucked her hands inside of her jacket pockets and said, "I saw you get beat up at school today."

"Just today?"

"A few times."

Rich nodded, but he no longer met Jenny's eyes. "Okay. Fair enough."

"I'm sorry I didn't do anything to help you."

"What could you have done?"

"Something." Jenny shrugged. "It wouldn't have mattered. Anything."

Rich nodded. "You're right, though. It wouldn't have mattered."

Jenny watched him. If there was maybe a moment when the Karma and the circles binding the universe were right and she might have helped him, it had passed. He turned away and continued down the steps. Jenny called after him, "See you in school tomorrow, okay?"

Rich didn't answer. Maybe he didn't even hear. He reached the corner, turned, and was gone.

Jenny looked back at the Civic Center. Someone inside was begining to switch down lights, so she turned and finished walking down the steps. She couldn't help Rich, she couldn't help herself, and as far as Maxwell Neuger went, she was sorry, but the arms race was currently out of her hands. What else could she do? She crossed the street and headed towards the bus stop.

There were three others already waiting for a ride, a gangly youth with a runny nose who was sucking on a beer and a couple leaning on each other by the lamp post. They would probably get off at any number of places along the route: Kessell Road, the apartment complex down by the K-Mart, or maybe even the Mall District. Jenny was almost certainly the only one who would be riding all the way out to the base. She leaned back against the wall of the corner appliance store to wait for the bus. The night was growing cooler, definite Montana weather, and none of the other people at the bus stop was talking.

Across the street was Dalton's Pets. They had declared it National Aquarium Month. A stack of tanks stood in the store window beneath colorful banners. Lights were set in the back, shining through and illuminating the fish as they danced.

Jenny turned away from them and began to button down.

Six

Rich followed Fourth Avenue South, the route that led directly to the base through what he called the Valley of the Dollar. The McDonald's was still open, but for drive-thru purchases only. The Taco Bell was closed, as was the Wendy's, the Paramount Video Store, and Patterson Real Estate. The Dairy Queen had completely shut down for the season.

He reached the longest stretch of the walk, the dark mill road which linked the outskirts of town to the access road to the base. Once past the last 7 Eleven, there was nothing except a small grey sign showing the way, a tavern frequented by people getting off work at the base, and the lights in the distance. At night the lights of Travers Air Force Base could be seen from any hilltop in Greylake.

As Rich walked in near total darkness towards the distant lights, he wondered about Jenny. Who was she?

He knew what her name was. He knew that she sat one row up and one aisle over in Mrs. Adams' class. He knew that she always looked good, got very good grades, and sometimes passed notes to Marcie Price. He also knew that she used to go with Kirk Mowry, who was also in class, but that now seemed to be over. Rich knew a lot of useless things about Jenny, but the real question remained: Who was she?

Why had she spoken to him in the hall today? Why had she spoken to him tonight? Why had she sat next to him? Why had she "needed" to talk to him?

It was enough to make a person crazy.

Rich walked on to the base.

The security policeman at the gate stepped out of his shack. He wore a blue beret and had a wary look. A plastic blue sign on the shack read, WELCOME TO TRAVERS AIR FORCE BASE, 633RD STRATEGIC MISSILE WING. PEACEKEEPER "AIRMAN FIRST CLASS TOWNE" ON DUTY.

The guard blocked Rich's path. A radio on his waist crackled, and he adjusted the rifle on his shoulder as Rich produced his ID card. Military Identification of Dependent. A piece of yellow laminated cardboard that says I am an adequate enough person to pass through this portal onto the great and legendary rock.

The SP nodded at Rich's picture and stepped back into his shack, out of the breeze.

Welcome home, Rich said to himself, relishing the coolness of the breeze. Chill me to the bone. Make me shiver right into my socks. Perhaps we could even arrange an illness, miss a few days of school. Wouldn't that be a pity. Rich slowed his pace. Base housing was located just inside the main gate, and he didn't live far. There was absolutely no hurry.

Turning onto the road where he lived, Rich walked past an empty house which stood bare at the corner. No curtains in the windows, which meant that even at night he could look right through the house into the streetlamp-lit backyard. Some people are like that, he thought. You could look right through them if you wanted to. Am I like that? Is that what Jenny was trying to do?

In his mind, Rich paused at the house. Every empty house on the base meant a new family moving in, probably transferring from overseas. Sometimes a new girl would show up in a class at school, and Rich would contemplate and hesitate, and then the opportunity would be lost. By then, she would have been informed of his infamous reputation and would watch him with different eyes. Rich longed for the day when his father would receive another assignment. That was the only advantage of the moves. Sometimes you lost all your friends, and sometimes you got the chance to start your whole life

51

over again. It wasn't going to happen, though. Graduation was too close and reassignments for enlisted missile maintenance technicians few and far between. They had been at Travers almost five years, and the Air Force was saving money by not moving people. One of the principal victims of this seemed to be Rich McFadden.

And so . . . home again.

Rich sighed. No matter how far you took yourself, or why you went in the first place, the rubber band would only stretch so far before it snapped you right back again. He went inside.

Gus was seated in the dimly lit living room watching a comedy show on television. Good. Gus never laughed much. Rich shut the door and stood behind his father's chair, waiting. "Where were you?" Gus asked.

"At the library."

"All this time?"

Rich blinked. "Not on base. Downtown."

Gus snorted. "You shouldn't read so much. You'll wind up blind." He reached for his beer, but found it empty.

Rich felt as though he should apologize. "Sorry."

"Get me another beer and go to bed."

Rich went to the kitchen, grabbed a can and delivered it, then went upstairs. He removed the tape seal from his door and confronted the brown inside. Closing the door, he thought about Lonerman. And his notebook. *Lonerman's Notebook* was Rich's infrequently kept journal. Rich felt perpetually guilty about that, and although he usually failed to remember any particular day's events, he often took the time to reduce an entire week to one wry line scratched on a Friday afternoon or late Saturday night. The comments didn't vary much: "Another loser," said one. "Another week, another useless series of depressions," said another. Sometimes, though, he took the trouble to try to explain what was bothering him. That was when things really got bogged down. It was better when he wasn't specific, as when he wrote, *I fear that God is an elected office, and I'm not registered to vote.*

Rich had to admit that most of the journal was close

52

to incoherent, but he figured that was probably for the best. Less stuff to blackmail him with should some thief break in and escape with it into the night.

Rich slipped out of his jacket and let it fall atop a pile of books at the bottom of his closet. As he neared his bed, he thought to make a grab for his journal, but he figured he would just mess things up. He should write about the goals of Stop the Nightmare, but he knew that wouldn't work. Whatever he tried to compose now would be reduced to a page or more of scrawled babble on the subject of how a pretty girl had talked to him and, more importantly, *why*.

Who was she? Rich searched his book pile, but her picture was not in his sophomore yearbook. He discarded the yearbook and sat on his bed, pulling his shoes off. He had thought of attending the STN meeting as the first step in his plan of political awakening and moral responsibility. What he had not counted on was seeing anyone from school there. He had assumed that nobody else would have the nerve or reason to show up. He tossed away his last sock. No doubt by second bell the news of another Rich McFadden flip-out would be all over school.

Who was she?

Rich pulled a shoebox full of cassette tapes from beneath the corner of his bed and sorted through it. He chose one and stuck it into his small tape player, keeping the volume low so as not to attract Gus. The tape player was a few years old, and one of the speaker wires seemed loose, but the slow ballad came across smooth and soothing. Rich didn't really care for hard rock.

Should he write anything in his journal this evening? And if so, what?

He took only a moment to decide.

No way.

Rich stood up in his bedroom and decided to leave his journal at the bottom of whatever pile it was now in. No point in recording any of today's madness, not Jenny, not school, none of it. He liked to keep track of things, but he was not so stupid as to believe that he was going to sit down years later and have a good laugh over them.

He figured that the experience with Lisa in world history had probably been the fifty-third worst thing that had ever happened to him in his life, but that the actual assault by Longhair was way down there, certainly ranking no higher than 163 or 164.

What about Jenny? Should he compile a list of the best things that had ever happened in his life?

No. Not if he expected to maintain a correct train of thought.

Rich closed his eyes. The world was run by people, and people could be the ones to change it. If they were willing to focus their attention.

Unfortunately, most of them were not.

He lay flat on his belly on the bed and reached into a pile of magazines beside the bed. He came out with a fairly recent copy of *Sports Illustrated*. In truth, he was interested in the pro football season, but there was nothing to be gained by letting anyone find out about that. He finished an article on the playoff prospects, tossed it aside, and extinguished the light.

His digital clock radio glowed in the dark.

12:42 AM.

Seven hours and eighteen minutes until school started.

What was he going to do until then?

Seven

Jenny stopped off at Marcie's house early the next morning and told her to skip breakfast. Marcie hobbled back from answering the door and collapsed into a chair, fighting with a shoe. The outcome of the battle was uncertain. Jenny noted that, as always, Marcie's socks didn't match. One was green, the other red. Jenny paced in front of her chair, clutching her books tightly. "We can grab some donuts or something at the canteen. I want to get started early."

Marcie frowned and glanced back towards the kitchen, where metal pots were clattering. She looked at Jenny. "My mom's making French toast. Do you know how often she actually makes it out of bed to fix me breakfast?"

"Tell her we have to go in early."

"Aren't we going to wait for the bus?"

Jenny shook her head. "I want to walk."

"You're crazy."

"Please."

Marcie hesitated just another second, then shrugged. "Can I take a peek at your algebra first? I didn't have time to finish mine."

Jenny nodded. She was used to the request, as Marcie rarely found the time to finish her algebra. Jenny reached into her book and handed the paper over. "Give it back to me at lunch. Can we go now?"

"You really are in a hurry."

"Yes."

Marcie finished lacing up her shoe. She stood up. "I

guess I need the exercise anyway. Let me grab my heavy coat." She went to the living room closet and pulled out her knee-length grey coat. She yelled to her mother that she was leaving. Her mother barely had time to raise a complaint before Marcie and Jenny disappeared out the front door.

"I'll be hearing about that after school," Marcie said.

"Blame it on me," Jenny responded.

"I always do."

The sky threatened rain. Not verbally, but all the other signs were there: dampness, a lingering overcast, brisk winds. Occasionally a gust would feel almost warm, but it was a deceitful wind, and the return of the chill was consistent enough to make the fur-lined windbreaker Jenny was wearing seem very inadequate. She was annoyed with herself for being in such a hurry that she had not bothered to look for anything warmer. It was the only thing Jenny had picked up from the Cockroach Woman, who was an absolute nut on health matters. Jenny's mother had not been. She had loved to dance in the rain.

They cut across a neighboring front lawn to reach the corner. As Marcie finished buttoning up her jacket, Jenny asked, "So what happened with Patty?"

Marcie looked at Jenny and shrugged. "What do you mean?"

"Did she come over to your house last night?"

"Yeah. She wanted to use my phone to call Brian."

"And? Did she call him?"

"Yeah. He even asked her out."

"Is she happy?"

"She's crazy. She told him no."

"What?"

Marcie rolled her eyes. "Part of the game."

Jenny said nothing. They crossed the street, and she asked, "So what about you?"

"What?" Marcie frowned. "You mean Dave?"

"Yeah."

"Well, I think I'm going to ask him out. Is that bad?"

"I don't think it is. I guess that depends on him."

Marcie asked about the afternoon before. "Was Amy

annoyed when you didn't come straight home after school?"

"Oh, yeah," said Jenny. "Her brain boiled. She had hot steam coming out of her ears." Then Jenny told Marcie where she had gone afterward.

"You did what?" Marcie shrieked, pulling her wind-blown hair out of her face. They were crossing the road opposite the post office. "You cannot be serious."

"It was really interesting. I was a little surprised myself. There are a lot of things you don't know, Marcie."

Marcie nodded, her square wire-rims falling down her nose now. "Yeah, I bet there are. But when your dad finds out you went to a Stop the Nightmare meeting, you are going to get it."

Jenny shrugged. "What can he do? Take away my birthday?"

Marcie pushed her glasses back into place and fixed her hair again. "This is another one of your 'Hate Me' tricks, isn't it?" They were walking past the Base Exchange parking lot now, as it was faster than walking all the way to the corner intersection. This meant they passed by the chapel and its fifteen KEEP OFF THE GRASS BY ORDER OF THE INSTALLATION COMMANDER signs.

Jenny was shaking her head, but Marcie kept up, saying, "Yeah, that's what it is, isn't it?" Marcie really frowned now. "Why do you spend so much time trying to make them hate you? First you complain that they don't love you enough, and then you get into these weird moods and you start—"

"You think that my being against nuclear war is some kind of weird mood? Some kind of annoying little game I want to play?"

Marcie nodded. "When your dad is a missile launch officer, it probably is."

Jenny shook her head. "I don't play those 'Hate Me' games anymore."

"Do you still write suicide notes?"

Jenny hesitated. She really hated to be pinned down for one odd habit. "Not for a while," she said.

"Are you still calling Amy the Cockroach Woman?"

"There's a reason for that."

"You never told me the reason."

Jenny stopped walking. They were still seven blocks from school, but there was plenty of time. "Okay. Cockroach Woman story all in one. Ready?"

Marcie fought with her hair. "I am nothing but ears."

Jenny nodded. "See, she hates bugs—all bugs. But she can't tolerate bug sprays or insecticides because they interfere with what she calls the 'natural order' of things. So she spends this unnatural amount of time crawling around the house on all fours laying out baking soda bombs for the roaches."

"Baking soda bombs?"

"Yeah. Supposedly, roaches can't burp. They can't relieve gas from inside their bodies. So if they munch down on baking soda, this gas builds up inside their body until they burst. The Cockroach Woman spends a lot of her time wiring up our house so that it'll be full of exploding cockroaches." Jenny smiled. "And that is where she got her name." She adjusted her books and started walking again.

Marcie followed. They were crossing Goddard Avenue. "Are you sure that's the only thing bothering you?"

Jenny considered that.

She considered the plight of that other miserable person in the world and wondered what his or her current status was. She thought about Rich in the middle of a lot being beaten up. She thought about the Cockroach Woman killing her fish and accusing her mother of being dead and gone. She thought about Maxwell Neuger and her dream the night before where the nuclear war was real, and the man who was launching the missiles was Captain Daddy . . .

She thought about all the things in the world that poetry couldn't answer for. Then she said, "Why should anything be bothering me? I can handle my life, already. I'm flexible. But that roach stuff, Marcie. It's just gross!"

Marcie nodded. "Well, you know it's not unusual for a kid not to appreciate a stepmother."

58

"All I want is to be left alone."

"Okay. So why did you go to the meeting last night?"

"I'm worried about the world."

Marcie shook her head. "Jenny, I've read some of your suicide notes. You wouldn't care if the entire world was boxed up and mailed to Cleveland."

Jenny shrugged. "I was interested."

They walked a little farther. Jenny consulted her watch. It was seventeen minutes until eight and they were nearing the school. Jenny was right on time, every second accounted for. Good. Then the large brick building loomed, and Jenny suddenly felt like pulling back. Turning around and going home, or going somewhere that felt like home. She looked at Marcie. "We've got a lot of friends, don't we?"

Marcie looked confused. "What do you mean?"

"I mean we have a lot of friends. We're both in the RT club, we've got Patty, some guys. A lot of guys. We have a lot of friends, right?"

"Okay," agreed Marcie. "So?"

"Do you ever feel lonely?"

Marcie hesitated. They were almost at school. She finally nodded. "Sometimes."

Jenny sighed. She didn't have to say anything. They had arrived at the Travers Air Force Base High School, complete with its required complement of hustlers, slackers, and the lost. Scattered about outside, some were smoking, some jabbering, some just viewing the day ahead with dread. It was a "Game Day," and the football players were all wearing their red dress jerseys beneath their letter jackets while cheerleaders shivered with tightly wrapped coats pulled down over short pleated skirts. A pep rally was scheduled for last hour, and many students were already plotting their escape.

"So what was the point about being lonely?" Marcie asked as they merged with the crowd.

"You know Rich McFadden?"

"No."

"He gets beat up a lot ... ?"

Marcie thought a second. "That kid who flips out? Talks about Indians and peace and stuff?"

"Yeah. What do you think about him?"

"I don't."

"Do you think he's crazy?"

Marcie stopped and tugged at her left pants leg, revealing a mismatched green sock. "Who am I to call anyone crazy?"

"I'm serious."

"Why?"

"He was at the meeting last night too."

"Wait a minute," said Marcie. "Are you trying to meter yourself against Rich McFadden? If he went to the meeting and is crazy, does that make you crazy too? Is that the question?"

"I didn't say that."

"You don't say a lot of things, Jenny."

"What I meant to say is that you and I both have a lot of friends, and sometimes we still get lonely. What about the people without any friends?"

Marcie stared. "That's awfully deep for eight in the morning, Jenny. Sounds like a poem."

"Sorry."

"There's Patty."

Patty was tucked along the wall of the main building, beneath a window where the school secretary was watering a plant. Patty was wearing a suit: black slacks and coat, with a ruffled white shirt and a thin black necktie. Her blond hair hung across her shoulders in contrast. Her books were at her feet and she was reading a newspaper. Patty nearly always brought the morning paper with her to school. Sometimes her first hour teacher would have to take it away in order to get her to pay attention. Patty would always say, "I am useless without the news."

Jenny and Marcie walked over to stand beside her. Patty looked up. "Another tax increase is likely. How will we afford to live?"

"Marry into wealth," Marcie said.

Patty smirked. "Could you marry a rich geek?"

"If he let me take separate vacations."

60

Patty laughed and looked at Jenny. "Can I borrow your algebra? I know you finished it."

Jenny pointed to Marcie. "She has it."

"I'll copy it at lunch." Patty next jerked a thumb at Marcie, saying, "We have got to set aside some time to teach this one how to dress."

"Me?" exclaimed Marcie. "Where did you get the idea to wear a black suit? From an undertaker?"

"This is my slumming outfit. I wear it when I need to hang out with people who can't match their socks."

"I go by thickness."

Jenny interrupted. "I went to that meeting last night."

Patty looked surprised. Marcie remained quiet as Jenny told the story. When she had finished, Patty smirked and said, "Doesn't impress me."

"Why not?"

"It's a hopeless cause. I don't dwell on hopeless causes."

Jenny frowned again. "Why is it so hopeless?"

Patty folded her newspaper. "You should read more current events and less algebra. Those missiles are going to be out there until the dinosaurs come back. You think the Russians will ever get rid of theirs? No way. Neither will we. Besides," Patty said, "there isn't going to be a nuclear war anyway."

"I'm not so sure," Jenny responded.

"It'll never happen, and you shouldn't be worrying about it. We have more immediate concerns."

"What more immediate concerns?" asked Marcie.

"Tonight."

Jenny looked puzzled.

"The away game," said Patty. "Next week is Homecoming, and tonight is Billings East. You do remember that we have a school football team, don't you?" Patty was smirking because Jenny and Marcie were both members of the RT pep club. The name RT was taken from the initial letters of the German words Roten Teufal, meaning "Red Devil." The nickname of the Travers High School football team was the Red Devils.

"Absolutely everybody is going to be there," Patty said.

Jenny grimaced. "We haven't won a game all year."

"Who cares? Billy Brooks is bringing beer."

"Where did you hear this?"

"Never mind."

"Are we supposed to sneak you on the RT bus again?" asked Marcie.

Patty smiled deviously. "I've got the car."

"What?" Marcie looked shocked. Billings was a two hour drive from Greylake, which meant a total of four hours on the road. Almost two hundred miles round trip. There was no way Patty's father, the Wing Commander, would allow that.

"Ah," said Patty. "Dear old Daddy is TDY as of this morning. Off to California and he took Mom with him."

"And they just left you here by yourself?" Jenny said.

"Why not? I'm completely trustworthy."

"You're going to drive all the way to Billings and back?"

"We can take turns."

"You're crazy."

Patty smiled.

The first bell rang. Patty tucked away her newspaper, and Marcie reached down and handed her books up. "We can plan it all at lunch," Patty said.

Marcie asked a question about Brian and the night before, but Jenny wasn't listening as Patty cackled her answer. She was trying to shake her first impression of the planned journey to Billings. Crowded in the bleachers, sitting quietly between people having a good time, spending the majority of the evening trying to distance herself. Why travel two hundred miles to be miserable when you could stay home and be miserable? Jenny dismissed the thought. Don't ruin good times planned by others. Some things just have to be tolerated in the name of a fun-filled youth.

Eight

Rich went down to the Stop the Nightmare office for one reason, and it had nothing to do with school. After all, how bad could a day at school be?

Not much worse than Friday had been, that was for sure.

After Longhair's attack the day before, the vultures moved in. He arrived at school that morning and went straight for his locker to get his books for world history. He spun the combination lock; it didn't open. That was funny. He tried once more—still nothing. A pimply freshman leaned in beside Rich. "Bad memory?" he asked. Rich didn't answer. Taking a breath, he fumbled with his wallet and pulled out the slip of paper he kept just for such an emergency.

Wait a second. This was strange. The combination written down was the same one he'd been dialing. He tried again.

That was when the snickers exploded behind him like cluster bombs. Rich couldn't even turn around to see who it was. They had pulled the old switched combo lock ploy on him, he realized with a sinking feeling in the pit of his stomach. Eventually, the custodian was summoned to clip the lock, and Rich had to play pack mule, lugging his books around with him all day.

But Rich could survive the nonsense, he knew that. He lived with it almost every day. What finally sent him down to the Stop the Nightmare office that Friday night was a phone call he tried to make. To a girl. Rich had called a girl on the telephone only once before in his life: Melissa Yeager, who sat directly behind him in seventh grade social studies class. Melissa had straight brown hair that reached midway down her back. Rich spent four long months working up the courage to make that call. There was a mixer scheduled, and he was pretty sure that she had no one to go with. He slipped upstairs with the phone book and sorted through the Yeager listings. There were four, and he called three before Melissa came to the phone.

Melissa was cheerful. Melissa was polite.

Melissa was not at all interested.

She said she considered him a friend but didn't want to "get serious." Rich translated that immediately: She didn't want to get serious with *him*.

He had never worked up the nerve to call a girl again.

This time, though, Rich had an angle. First of all, this Jenny girl did seem interested, even if she had strange motives for speaking to him—as she had indeed spoken to him again that very day. Secondly, if rejected, he could make it seem as though he only called to ask a question about Stop the Nightmare. He could use the peace organization as a shield. He wasn't really calling for himself; he was calling for the world. What could she say?

Just no. All she could say was no.

Rich dragged the upstairs hall telephone into his room and secured the door behind him. He felt an odd excitement as he sat on the edge of his bed and, hesitantly, began to flip through the white pages of the phone book. He recognized the feeling immediately. It was identical to the one he experienced when he knew Longhair was searching for him and somehow he managed to get away. The thrill of escape.

He found the number, the only Westphal listed on Travers AFB, and he dialed without hesitation. Bold, aren't we?

"Hello?"

It was a woman's voice.

Rich managed to speak. "Is Jenny there?"

"Hold on a second."

But the voice that spoke next was a man, and Rich

wasn't prepared. It was Jenny's father, and he started speaking right away. "Kirk? I need to talk to you about Jenny. She already left for the game, but could you stop by tommorow?"

Rich dropped the phone.

Stupid, stupid, stupid . . .

One question: Was it supposed to hurt like this? Rich shuddered. The house was empty, Mike was gone—even Mom and Dad were off somewhere—so there wasn't a lot of reason to stay home. Mom had left that money so he could go to a movie, but there was something about going to a movie alone on Friday night that gave him the chills. Every couple in the theater mocked you without even meaning to.

He knew he was thinking too much about Jenny. He had destroyed himself like this before, misinterpreting the attention of some girl. It was self-inflicted torture, but at the same time there was that thrill . . . of escape. Yes, the thrill that would be there until he found out for sure she didn't like him. Then the thrill would develop sharp edges.

To take his mind off of Jenny, Rich started thinking about Stop the Nightmare.

Rich knew one thing about life: Some thoughts were more pointless than others. He had no idea how late the STN office was open on Friday night, but he knew it was at least a valid destination. And that was something he hadn't had in a long time. A valid destination.

So he went. The street was dark, and the banner on the left front window read, SAVE THE CHILDREN. The one on the right said, STOP THE NIGHTMARE.

Between the two windows was a glass door, decorated with stickers. The office used to be a store of some kind; Rich couldn't remember what.

Music came from within.

Rich stood there a moment, feeling shy and embarrassed in a weird way. What if they dismissed him as just a kid? How stupid would he feel then? What if they were like cultists, wanting to brainwash him to sell flowers at intersections? What if they just didn't like him?

Let no pain be self-induced, thought Rich. I'm going

65

in. But his last thought wasn't about STN; it was about Jenny, and he felt bad because of it. In a way, he figured, Jenny had betrayed a strange confidence between them. It was nothing she had or hadn't done, only that before she started talking to him he had almost adjusted to his lot in life. Almost.

Now he felt lonely again, all the time.

So he went inside.

A man Rich recognized as Reverend Mark Lowell was carrying a box from a back room to a shelf by the front window. He looked up as Rich entered and smiled. "Well, hi there!"

Rich was a little startled by the enthusiasm. He nodded back.

"How are you tonight?"

Rich shrugged. "I don't know."

Reverend Lowell laughed. "Well, at least you're honest. That's refreshing."

Rich nodded. "Is it?"

Reverend Lowell stopped laughing. He set the box down and looked Rich over closely. "Yeah, it is."

"Sorry."

A woman came out of the backroom laughing. She had short, pixie-cut dirty blonde hair. She said, "I see you have found assistance, Reverend."

Reverend Lowell shrugged. "I don't know yet, Karen." He looked at Rich. "Have I found assistance here?"

"What do you need done?"

"The list goes on and on. What's your name?"

"Rich."

"Richard?"

"Rich."

Reverend Lowell nodded. "Got it. Are you interested in helping out, Rich?"

"I guess."

"You guess? Either you are or you aren't."

"I am, yeah."

"Good."

The front door opened behind Rich and several people came in, a guy and two girls, carrying two bags from an

66

ice cream shop and several cones. They, too, were laughing, and one of the girls said, "Oops, we didn't get enough."

"Maxwell, we have volunteers," Reverend Lowell said.

"Volunteers is plural," said the guy holding the ice cream shop bag.

"Yes, and hope springs eternal. Meet Rich."

The guy handed the ice cream shop bag to one of the girls and reached to shake Rich's hand. "Got a last name?"

"McFadden."

"Good. I'm Max Neuger."

"From the meeting."

"I'm the loudmouth, yeah." He turned back to the girls. "Time out a second. Rich, this motley crew is Kris and Valerie."

Reverend Lowell jumped in. "Yeah, and I forgot to introduce Karen here, or Tammy. She's still out back."

"Better tell her the ice cream is melting."

"Rich?" asked one of the girls. She had long black hair and a round face. With a few changes she might have been Jenny years later. Max had introduced her as Valerie. "Hungry for ice cream?"

Rich shook his head. "No, thanks."

"You sure? We've got extra. I'm a piggie and I always buy two."

"I'm a diabetic."

Max turned, looking very serious. "Are you kidding?"

Rich shrugged. "Yeah, I am kidding. Sorry."

"Don't be sorry; I can appreciate a good comeback."

"I'm glad somebody can," Rich said morosely.

Max laughed. "Sounds like Rich here has the same problem as everybody else."

Rich watched as they started to eat their ice cream. He asked, "What problem is that?"

"Trouble at home."

Rich didn't say anything.

They seemed glad to have the extra set of hands. The electricity had just been switched on that very day, and they were still in the process of clearing debris, hanging posters, and moving furniture in and around. Rich was just happy to be there. Reverend Lowell urged them on,

67

and Max charted the course, like the captain and first mate of a fast frigate. Kris was a pretty girl who had blonde frizzy hair, wore a baggy sweater, and flirted with Max. Valerie and Tammy, it turned out, were students from the college in town, and they spent a good part of the time chatting at Rich, trying to get him to taste their ice cream cones. They giggled, and Rich felt tall, because the giggles were fun and not aimed at him. Karen, the first girl to emerge from the backroom, was super friendly and asked a lot of questions. It was she who discovered he was from the base.

Max was listening, hanging a poster. He had just bruised his arm but shrugged it off. "So what's so surprising about that?" he asked.

Karen shrugged. "Just seems weird. Son of a jetter." *Jetter* was a term for people from the base.

"They're just people," said Max, rubbing his bruise. "At least some of them are."

Karen smiled, changing the subject. Sort of. "What does your dad do at the base?"

"Maintenance."

"Maintenance?"

"He's in one of the missile shops."

"Oh." Karen nodded. She handed Max up another poster. "So does he work in weapons, or on delivery systems?"

Rich blinked. "What?"

Even Max frowned from his stepladder. "What difference does it make?"

Karen defended herself. "I know a guy from the office who works in the 221st missile shop, but he's in guidance systems. I thought Rich might know him."

"Why?" Rich was still confused. "How would I know him? I don't work in the shop. My dad does."

Karen smiled, steering the conversation again. She talked a lot and seemed to care about everything. She told Rich she worked as a secretary in a real estate office and had been one of the first to volunteer after the meeting the night before. Rich decided not to let that pass.

68

Maybe he could figure out if his own reasons were valid. He asked her, "Why?"

Karen looked at him blankly. "What?"

"So why did you volunteer? Why are you here?"

"I . . . I guess I have to be here."

"Is that really a reason?"

"I think it is."

"Okay."

Karen now seemed suspicious. "Okay? Okay what?"

"Okay, I guess you're right."

Karen didn't say anything else. She went into the back room for something. Max was suddenly beside Rich, saying, "That's a pretty good question."

Rich glanced over.

"Got an answer?"

Rich thought about it. "You ever watch old Gary Cooper movies?"

"All I can."

"*Beau Gest.*"

"The French Foreign Legion."

"Yeah."

"So that's why you're here? To forget yourself?"

Rich shrugged. "Maybe. So why are you in this?"

"That's privileged information."

"How do you earn the privilege?"

Max smiled. Maybe he couldn't help it. He said, "Watch the movie again. I'm in there somewhere."

"You are?"

"Sure. Isn't everybody?"

Rich started to say something. Maybe he felt almost comfortable enough to ask a question, to bring Jenny's name into it, to probe for some advice. Maybe it wasn't that at all. It didn't matter. Because that was the second the world chose to—

—Crash!

Shards of glass exploded, razor sharp splinters flying. Rich would have sworn later that the lights blinked, but that was impossible. Outside a car was screeching away, tires squealing, as something, a brick, clumped hard against the back wall. Glass tinkled. Rich looked around quickly.

Nobody seemed to be hurt, and Max was outside in an instant. Kris had screamed, but now Tammy was calming her. Valerie and Karen were huddled with Reverend Lowell. Max wandered back into the store. "Well, it's started," he said.

Rich looked at him.

Max sighed. "It's an old line."

Rich nodded again.

"God save those who do, from those who don't."

Nine

Dreaming again, Jenny heard voices. A slamming of doors. The sound swelled, hundreds of voices, all shouting a message she didn't understand. She struggled against the noise, turned from it, bolted, trying to run. *Don't go in the bathroom.* What? What? *Don't go in the bathroom.* Why?

There's a razor in the bathtub . . .

Jenny awoke in her room, heart pounding. It was dark, and she instinctively held her breath. What had happened now?

The silence of the house numbed her senses.

Not a sound. It was late. Twenty minutes before five, according to the hands of the Hairy Werewolf.

Jenny began to breathe again, trying to relax. False alarm. No razors in the bathtub. No screaming. Years before, Jenny used to awaken to crashing glass downstairs. She used to race down and try to stop the fighting. Until she realized she couldn't ever stop the fighting. Until the fighting stopped on its own. Then came the Cockroach Woman and everything she had to deal with now. Jenny sat up, out of habit balling herself up in the corner of her bed against the wall, bracing herself against the wall. The reflex system had remained with her, and she still often woke from a deep sleep at the slightest unusual sound.

Jenny measured her breaths out evenly now, relaxing. Button down. Nobody was fighting downstairs, and even if they were, who cares? That isn't Mom. It's the Cockroach Woman. Mom wanted to dance in the rain, so she left.

She just up and left.

Fine. It was probably the best move. I should go too. Isn't that what I'm thinking all the time?

Jenny rolled herself out of bed and walked into the bathroom. When she came back to her room, she closed the door behind her and switched on the light. Leaning back against the door, she closed her eyes and thought again about that other miserable person in the world. Hello? Are you awake for me? I cannot sleep.

By rights, Jenny presumed that she ought to be tired. She hadn't crawled into bed until almost three. Fortunately, the Cockroach Woman hadn't found out; Captain Daddy was, as always, in the missile field. If necessary, though, Jenny figured she could answer for it to Captain Daddy. Just another one of those things that couldn't be helped.

In the interest of a fun-filled youth?

Hardly.

The evening was as close to a total catastrophe as possible without actual arrests being made. The trip to Billings had been uneventful, although Patty drove her father's red Ford Escort at speeds that terrified Jenny. They found the Billings East stadium with little difficulty, but so had many others, including some people Jenny had no desire to see. Early in the first quarter Kirk came squeezing through the bleacher section where Jenny, Patty, and Marcie were seated. Kirk was dragging Roger Krowitz with him. Roger smiled at Patty and tried to strike up a conversation. Patty ignored him. Kirk paused in front of Jenny and gave a little wave. "Hi."

Jenny looked up and, as passively as she could manage, said, "Hello."

Kirk looked hurt for only a minute, then pulled on his casual smile. "You guys take it easy." He addressed all three of them, as if he had not meant to speak only to Jenny in the first place. Shoving a hand into Roger's back to get his attention, Kirk started down the row. Jenny watched them go.

Marcie, who was drinking from a soda with no ice, said, "I hate Roger Krowitz."

"Too bad about Kirk, though." Patty shrugged.

Jenny looked over at Patty, but Patty had nothing else to say. She just shook her head. Jenny turned her attention back to the game. The Red Devils were being routed, as always. They were down by two touchdowns and a two-point conversion at halftime, when Patty and Marcie decided to follow Billy Brooks and Rick Waters out to their car. Since Patty represented The Ride Home, Jenny went with them.

Things began to deteriorate.

Paul Lacey and some friends of his were also out in the parking lot, and a few of them wandered over to the party that was starting at the trunk of Billy Brooks' Chevrolet Impala. Jenny was more than apathetic enough about Paul Lacey, but he seemed very enthusiastic about her. He sat opposite her in algebra and always seemed to have a question he needed her help with. Paul was tall and so skinny that Jenny felt sure he was suffering from some obscure form of malnutrition. He wore a sleeveless denim jacket, and his crooked smile made Jenny increasingly nervous. Besides that, he was already drunk.

Paul leaned on the mirror of the passenger-side door and popped the top of another beer can. "You don't know this, but I think smart girls are great," he slurred. "I've always respected you especially, on account of your smart mind."

Patty brought Jenny a beer from the trunk of the car, but Jenny declined. Paul tried to encourage her. "Go for it."

"No."

"Chicken?" asked Patty with a sly smile.

Jenny frowned. "Somebody has to drive you home."

Patty shrugged, opening the beer for herself. "I think it's absolutely essential that you relax."

"I'm relaxed. Don't I seem relaxed?"

"No."

"Maybe I'm not then. Who can tell?"

Patty just shook her head.

73

Marcie, who had at first been hesitant, now stood at the back of the car, working on her second beer and talking to Billy and Rick. Patty took another sip of her beer and went back to join them. Paul smiled again and continued creeping up on Jenny. She continued backing away.

The stadium public address system was audible in the parking lot, and they heard weak clapping when the Red Devils finally scored, although the points were rendered meaningless when Billings East returned the kickoff for another touchdown. Travers was being thrashed again.

"Why don't we go out sometime?" Paul asked.

Jenny was running out of polite ways to say no.

"We could go to a concert in Helena or something . . ."

Jenny shook her head. "I'm going with somebody."

Paul frowned. "You and Kirk broke up. I know you ain't going with anybody."

"I didn't say it was Kirk, did I?"

"No? Okay. Who are you going with?"

Jenny hesitated only a second. "Rich McFadden."

Paul looked at her blankly. "Who?"

Jenny repeated, "Rich McFadden."

Paul was obviously trying to fit the name to a face. "McFadden? You don't mean flip-out McFadden, the punch-bag?"

Jenny didn't answer.

Paul stepped back. "Excuse me for telling you this, but Rich McFadden is sort of like the world-class geek of all time . . ."

Jenny turned away from him. He muttered something else, then moved away. Jenny just shrugged it off. Anything to stay out of trouble.

Midway through the fourth quarter, Marcie had a junior league freakout and stormed off somewhere with Billy Brooks in pursuit. Jenny wanted to go after her, but Patty told her not to bother. "It's absolutely essential we let this girl figure out what she wants from life."

"Wants?" said Jenny. "I think she wants to go home, like I do."

Patty just shook her head and had another beer.

Courdray Zimmerman came over about then, part of

74

the party of course, and suggested that he and Jenny climb into the front seat of the car "just to keep warm." Jenny had a hard time avoiding him. Whenever she moved around to the back, he followed, and whenever she made it to the front, he was there. Finally, she stood her ground and told him to back off.

He looked as if he had been slapped, which was to be Jenny's next move, if necessary. "What?" he said.

"Just leave me alone. Okay?"

Courdray tossed his beer can away and muttered an expletive in farewell. Jenny watched him go. Marcie returned just after eleven o'clock. Whatever had upset her had definitely been reconciled, and now it was confirmed: Marcie and Billy were going to Homecoming together. Jenny was talking to Patty when Marcie made her announcement. Jenny said, "What about Dave Meely?"

Marcie looked flustered for just a second, then she exploded in a giggle. "He's a geek!"

Jenny just nodded. Geeks obviously deserved whatever bad things happened to them. Or so was the prevalent line of thinking. And one day, she told herself, we will all wake up as geeks in somebody's eyes.

An hour or so later Jenny finally convinced a very trashed Patty and Marcie that it was time to head back, but when they located the red Escort there was yet another surprise. One of the rear tires was flat.

"No problem," said Billy Brooks, who had followed. "I'll drive you guys home."

"No way," said Jenny.

"It's okay, I'm fine. I haven't really been drinking."

"Define 'haven't really' for me."

Patty shook her head, looking a little wilted. She was leaning on the trunk. "We can't leave the car. Daddy would crucify me."

Jenny sighed. "Okay. I'll change the tire."

Billy shrugged. "Do what you have to do."

Patty fumbled in her purse for the trunk keys. Jenny took them and, since nobody was really in any condition to help her, she changed the tire by herself. It took over half an hour, and she got quite dirty doing it, since the

75

spare was covered in motor oil. Patty watched with some concern as she finished up, and as Jenny was lowering the car from the jack, she saw why. Patty began to get sick.

Served her right, Jenny thought vengefully. Then she felt bad. She went to help, but Patty, who was doubled over and making gagging noises behind the car, waved her off. Finally she stumbled back some, tried to make a joke of it, and crawled into the back seat. Billy was holding Marcie and shaking his head. "Man, Patty is absolutely wasted."

"The whole night is wasted," Jenny said. Patty was already asleep, so Jenny slammed the jack back in the trunk, dragged Marcie from the clutches of Billy, and started back for Greylake.

It was almost twelve-thirty.

The roads were less traveled at that hour, fortunately, and they made pretty good time. Marcie fell asleep herself thirty minutes into the ride, and Jenny was all alone, with only the company of a static-filled radio. She drove home carefully, occasionally glancing at her sleeping friends. She wondered why they did it.

An answer occured to her as she neared Greylake.

Maybe that was the secret of avoiding insanity. Consider the world a party, and instead of constantly peeking in through a window, as she so often did, simply invite yourself in.

She drew a questioning glance from the security policeman at the main gate as she drove onto the base in the Wing Commander's car, but he waved her on. Marcie woke up enough to let herself in and avoid the hassle of waking her parents. Jenny drove Patty home, then walked across the base to her own house, sneaking in at twenty minutes until three in the morning. Ten minutes later she was asleep in her bed. Sleeping soundly, until the dream.

Awake now, leaning back against the door of her room and knowing what she was about to do, Jenny grew nervesick. She opened the door and started downstairs. At the bottom, she clicked the dim light on above the hall phone table and lifted the receiver. She put her hand over the phone to muffle the dial tone and consulted the directory for the area code. She dialed directory assistance for the Chicago, Illinois area.

There were six buzzing rings before a click. "Mrs. Phillips, what city please?"

Jenny hushed her voice, terrified at the prospect of being heard, of having to explain. "Chicago."

"What listing do you want?"

"Do ... Do you have a listing for a Barbara Louise Westphal?"

"Do you have an address?"

"It changes."

"One moment please." There was a sound of punching numbers, then, "I am sorry, I have no such listing."

"Wait!" Jenny said. She thought. "Radke. That's her maiden name. Barbara Louise Radke."

"No address on that either?"

"No."

"Still no listing."

Jenny thought desperately. Of course! "White. Barbara White."

"Barbara White?"

"My grandmother's maiden name."

"You want a listing for Barbara White?"

"Yes."

There was more clicking of numbers, and already Jenny felt disappointment and relief swelling at the same time. She was surprised when the operator said, "Yes, I have that number."

"You do?"

"Yes." The operator read it to Jenny, who scrawled it on the message pad by the telephone.

"Thank you."

Jenny hung up.

She looked at the telephone number written on the small white square of paper before she tore it up into tiny, undecipherable pieces. She tossed the pieces into the trash, but it was too late. She was too good with numbers.

She closed her eyes in the semi-darkness. How do you

77

go from being somebody who cries over everything to being someone who cries over nothing? That was the question, but here was the answer: You didn't. It was not possible. Some people just chose to weep on the inside.

What would she say if Mom answered? Hello? I miss you?

Sorry, wrong number?

"I didn't mean to bother you."

Jenny whispered out loud, but she hadn't dialed yet. Yet.

The phone was ringing before Jenny realized what she had done. Three rings, four. Hang up! There isn't anyone there, anyway. Nobody that you know. Hang up!

Hang on!

Every time you try this, you turn away from it. What are you afraid of learning? The real reason Mom went away? Why do you think Captain Daddy avoids the entire issue? Because you remind him of her. And she's gone.

Forever.

But maybe she is out there, waiting. Waiting for you to call so she can tell you the real reason. It wasn't Captain Daddy, or dancing in the rain. It was you. *You put the razor in the bathtub . . .*

"Hello?" answered a tired woman's voice.

Jenny hung up instantly.

What to say?

THE NEXT PART

Ten

There were no gaudy signs on the street proclaiming the area a nuclear free zone. In fact, the entire Stop the Nightmare operation seemed rather low-key. One of the picture windows was boarded up; the other had drawn blinds. Jenny recognized the shop as having previously been a toy and model store, and she might have passed it by completely had it not been for the sticker in the door proclaiming the World CND, Campaign for Nuclear Disarmament.

It was just after nine in the morning, another depressing Monday in November, Jenny thought. It was still cool outside, but at least the sun was shining. Occasionally someone would shoot past her to enter one of the other stores on Eighth Street, but so far she was the only one standing outside the Stop the Nightmare office, waiting for it to open for the day.

Was it even open on weekdays?

There were no operating hours posted. Jenny supposed it possible, even probable, that Maxwell Neuger had been unable to locate enough volunteers to go through with his ambitious plan to keep a public information center open every day. After all, nuclear disarmament was a pretty hysterical line of thinking, wasn't it? Us against the world, with either Us coming out on top or else the world blown to pieces. In the meantime things were bound to get rough. Maxwell Neuger had said that himself. Who would wish to throw himself into the fray?

As for herself, Jenny couldn't single out any specific

moment when she'd decided to cross the line into activism. She had attended the first meeting more or less on a whim.

She grimaced. More or less on a whim to see Maxwell Neuger again.

Jenny had been doing a lot of things on a whim lately. There had really been no plan to skip a day of school and offer her services to Stop the Nightmare. She had just sort of drifted over. It was like losing time. Your body started to operate on a purely mechanical level, following its pre-programmed instructions with no questions being asked. Exactly what set the program in motion no longer mattered.

Jenny had passed a note to Marcie in Homeroom telling her that she was leaving for the day. If anyone asked, Marcie was to say that Jenny had gotten sick and gone home. Marcie looked troubled, but nodded.

So here Jenny was, waiting outside in the cold. She checked her watch again, trying to keep an accurate track. Nine-fourteen.

Nine twenty-seven.

Nine thirty-four.

Empty minutes in between.

Obviously, nobody was going to show.

She stuffed her hands deep into her jacket pockets, trying to keep warm. She was wearing her faded brown pile-lined coat. Underneath she wore a baggy pink checkered long-sleeve shirt and light brown cotton dungarees with wide suspenders. She wore leg warmers low on her ankles so she could wear her low-topped shoes. She had wanted to look good for school today, for no particular reason. She—

Bogus.

Jenny chilled. She was cutting herself up again.

You had no intention of going to school today. Not for any longer than it took to pass the note to Marcie. You wanted to look good for *him.*

For whom?

Him. You know. The one with the eyes?

Button down.

82

Jenny glanced up and down the street once more before deciding it was time to leave. What do I do for the rest of the day, she wondered. Go back to school?

She was heading back down to the bus stop when she met up with him. The one with the eyes.

Maxwell Neuger was rounding the corner, burdened down with an overflowing brown paper sack. He was wearing a red down jacket with a ski lift pass still clipped to the zipper. He struggled with a ring of keys and the leash of a large dog. He smiled immediately when he saw Jenny. "Hey, hi! How are you?"

Jenny nodded. "Fine."

"Great! Can you help me out?"

"Sure." She sagged as soon as she took the bag from Neuger's arms. What was in it? A hundred pounds of bricks? The dog, a mixed-breed collie with a thick coat of red hair, tugged at the leash in Neuger's hand. "Sorry I'm so late," Neuger was saying. "I stopped off to pick up a few things. I remember you. You're Jenny, right?" He jammed the keys into the lock, twisted, and led the dog and Jenny inside. He dropped the leash and held the door open until Jenny cleared it, then he snapped it shut behind her. "The place isn't much, but the rent is cheap, and, well, we have high hopes."

Jenny stood there, holding the bag, waiting. She was feeling calm, very calm, but she wondered whether volunteer work was really her style.

"Set the bag on the floor, anywhere."

Jenny frowned at the dirty floor and sat the bag on top of one of the office's two desks. The office also had a small refrigerator, a wastepaper basket, and one lonely looking black telephone. The inside of the office had been declared a nuclear free zone. A large blue peace sign poster with bold red letters made it so. Posters covered every wall; that was the extent of the decorating. A map of the state was dotted with red bull's-eyes and labeled, "Target: MONTANA!" The same hollow-eyed children who had haunted the Civic Center adorned these walls, looking down and asking, WILL THERE BE A WORLD FOR US?

83

Neuger twisted around and asked, "It is Jenny, isn't it?"

"Yes."

He smiled. "Great. And since my father is much more comfortable with 'Mr. Neuger' than I am, I would appreciate it if you could call me Max."

Jenny nodded. Maxwell Neuger. Max. As though they were old friends. Max and Jenny. Jenny and Max.

"Eh?"

She smiled. "Max."

"Great." He looked down. "Ah, I see one more introduction is in order. This is Baxter." He reached down to scratch the dog's head. Baxter seemed to enjoy the attention and sat up, panting. "Baxter, this is Jenny. She's going to be helping us out. She is not lunch." Max explained to Jenny. "That's a little canine humor. Baxter's been with me almost five years. He even went to jail with me once."

Jenny frowned. "Jail?"

Max nodded, standing and moving to unpack the paper bag. "Yeah. I had old Baxter with me when I did the peace protest up at launch facility Romeo Twenty-nine at Malmstrom last year. They put me away for thirty days, and Baxter did the time in a Federal kennel. Sort of a slammer for dogs. Supervised, no doubt, by German shepherd police dogs."

"Didn't you know they'd put you in jail?"

Max started pulling sodas from the bag and stuffing them into the refrigerator. "I was counting on it," he said. "Making speeches isn't enough. We got out of Vietnam through protest, and that's the only way we'll ever get them to put the brakes on this arms race. I only worry that there won't be enough time."

Jenny nodded, noticing that it wasn't getting any warmer in the office. "Isn't there any heat in here?"

"I turned it on when I came in," Max said. "Sometimes it just takes a while to warm up."

Jenny jammed her hands back into her pockets. She felt uncomfortable just standing there. Max dug deeper into the bag's contents and pulled out a few boxes of cookies, some size D batteries, a portable radio. He plugged the batteries into the radio and clicked it on, looking for a station. Jenny smiled at him now. "You're feeling better."

"What?"

"The other night at the meeting you were sick."

Max shrugged it off. "Just a sore throat."

"You said it was your stomach. The cookies you ate."

Max finished playing with the radio and shrugged again. "Sick is sick, I guess."

Jenny watched as he pulled some envelopes from the desk drawer. She asked, "What did you mean about there not being enough time?"

Max flinched. Just a little. "All I meant was we have to move faster. Use more drastic measures."

"What kind of drastic measures?"

Max laughed. "Nothing violent, Jenny, I promise. I'm talking about civil disobedience."

"What's that?"

"Ever here about a guy named Gandhi?"

"No."

"India, 1948. The British still maintained India as a colony, and Gandhi and a lot of other Indians wanted their country back. They didn't want a bloody civil war, though, so Gandhi pressed what he called 'civil disobedience.' No violent reactions; they just stopped doing what they were told."

Jenny couldn't help looking confused.

"Remember Martin Luther King?"

"You mean civil rights? That sort of thing?"

Max nodded. "The sit-ins and marches of the 1960's. We could start now by maybe occupying another missile site. Maybe set up a peace camp somewhere. Do something to get the issue back on page one. Put some film on the six o'clock news."

"That sounds a little stupid." Jenny shocked herself by saying it.

Max stopped counting envelopes and looked up. "Why is that?"

"Wouldn't occupying a missile site be dangerous?"

Max shook his head. "Not really. The last thing the Air Force would want to do is shoot an unarmed civilian. The signs out there say 'deadly force is authorized', but they don't really mean it. That would just give us a martyr, and they don't want that."

Jenny frowned. "Do *we* want that?"

Max was still, his face frozen. His eyes, and the power they concealed, frightened Jenny. She was convinced that those eyes, when they were strong, could bend wills. Make others believe untrue things. She was suddenly feeling very shaky when a smile burst across Max's face. He nodded and said, "I remember you now. You sat in the back of the class and watched me the whole time."

Jenny looked away, embarrassed. "I'm not sure I want to go to jail for all of this."

Max stopped. "Well, I didn't mean you."

Jenny didn't say anything.

Max produced a roll of stamps from his pocket and pushed the envelopes forward. "Objective of the day," he said. "We have to address two hundred and fifty envelopes and mail out as many letters as fast as we can."

Jenny grimaced. For this she skipped school?

Max looked at Baxter and said, "Stand up and be a dog. Try and act like a professional canine for a change." The dog rose. Max turned back to Jenny. "It is really fantastic of you to help like this. Everybody acts concerned, but hardly anyone wants to commit."

"I'll commit, I'm just not sure how concerned I am," Jenny mumbled.

Max chewed on his lower lip. "We have to educate you." He gave Baxter a pat. "How are your parents going to feel about all this? I'm sure they won't like you skipping school."

Jenny shrugged. "Who knows?"

"You probably shouldn't do that much. What kind of work does your dad do at the base? Is he a contractor? A civilian?"

"No, he's Air Force."

"Yeah? What does he do?"

"He's a capsule jock."

86

Max stopped petting Baxter. "Missile launch officer?"

"Yeah."

Max let out a low whistle. "He'll have a nervous breakdown if he finds out you're helping us."

"Whatever."

Max was shaking his head. "Missile launch officer," he said again. "That's really wicked."

"That's his life."

Max absently tore into one of the bags of cookies, offering them over to Jenny. She took a couple of chocolate chips. Max ate one himself. "We had a kid come down Friday night. His dad is a Master Sergeant in one of the missile shops."

"What was his name?" Jenny nibbled on a cookie.

"What?"

"The other kid from the base."

"Oh, his name is Rich."

Jenny stopped eating. "McFadden?"

"Yeah, you know him?"

Jenny shrugged. That was a good question. On Friday night she had told someone she was going steady with Rich McFadden, but other than that, no. "We've got some classes together," she answered.

"He's going to help us out in the evenings."

"Doing what?"

"Whatever comes up."

Jenny ate another cookie. "So what's the big deal about my dad being a capsule jock? I mean, it's him, not me."

Max looked at her now, and his eyes were on fire again. "It's everything that scares us, Jenny. Someone who can push the button. Someone who will push the button."

Jenny had to look away. "It's cold in here."

Max let his voice calm. "Yeah. Look, it's probably no colder outside than it is here. I owe Baxter his morning run. Would you like to come? Maybe by the time we get back it'll be warmer."

"Where do you take him?"

"Terrace Park."

Jenny hesitated only a second. "I like the park."

"Great."

87

Baxter's leash was resecured, and they were off. Max took the time to relock the front door. He gestured to the boarded up window in explanation. "Not everybody in the neighborhood likes us."

The park was about seven blocks away, on the river, and the walk was pleasant enough. Once they arrived at the park, Baxter took off to chase the birds. He failed to catch any. The robins and wrens were gone for the season, the ducks escaped skyward, and the pigeons held their ground, snapping back.

Jenny and Max trailed after Baxter, walking along the edge of the pond which, fed by the river, was the anchor of Terrace Park. Max held the folded leash in his left hand and kept patting it against his leg as they walked. "Jenny, Jenny," he mused. "Yeah, that's a nice name, but doesn't anyone ever call you Jennifer?"

"Only the Cockroach Woman when she's mad."

"The who?"

Jenny hesitated. "My stepmother."

Max nodded. He didn't ask about it, and Jenny appreciated that. Finally Max said, "I think I should call you Jennifer."

"Why?"

"Because nobody else does. That's usually a good enough reason."

Jenny smiled. A squirrel appeared in front of Baxter, panicked and took off with Baxter in hot pursuit. Jenny said, "You're from Michigan."

"Yeah." Max folded the leash over again and stuck it in his jacket pocket. "I'm the outside agitator they brought in to shake things up."

"Who is 'they'?"

"STN."

"I thought you *were* STN."

Max laughed. "Reverend Mark Lowell is STN. The group has been around for almost two years, without much happening. Tea socials, that sort of thing. Reverend Lowell read about me getting busted up at Malmstrom last year, and he gave me a call."

"Why?"

Max hesitated for a moment. Jenny was amazed at the change since he spoke in her sociology class. Brown hair, tossed by the wind, fell casually into his eyes. He was still pale, but it was a relaxed lack of color. There was power beneath his surface. "That's easy enough," he said, smiling. "I started protesting at a SAC bomber base up around Lansing. That's in Michigan, back home. I got so involved I dropped out of college to keep it up. I came out with some people on a road trip to protest the missiles at Malmstrom last summer, up in Great Falls. Got arrested again, of course, same charge. Federal trespass. My parents didn't exactly welcome me back, their son the convicted Federal criminal. So when Reverend Lowell called, I figured ... Hey, why not? I'll go to jail for a living."

"Go to jail for a living?"

"Yeah. STN pays my way, organizes a protest, a demonstration or two. Usually somebody winds up crossing the line, and usually that somebody is me."

Jenny stopped walking. Baxter was far ahead, nipping at something. Jenny asked, "Isn't that going to get you into some serious trouble someday?"

"Not really. The Federal Magistrate usually lets me plead guilty on the spot. Suspended sentence." Max bent for a pebble and flipped it at the pond. "Last year was the first time I ever actually had to do any time. Weird. I still don't know why it worked out that way."

Jenny looked towards the water. "Is that why you're here? Not to make speeches and stuff, but to go to jail when they want you to?"

Max didn't answer.

"Max?"

Finally he spoke. "Walt Whitman once said, 'Obey little, resist much.' Does that help you out any?"

Jenny thought about it. "Does somebody always have to go to jail for the cause?"

"Sometimes somebody has to do more than that."

Eleven

A week went by quickly. When Rich got home after school on Friday the twenty-second, he found the house quiet except for the greeting mews of Logan, the cat. Rich heard the pattering of paws on the tile floor, and the grey striped animal met him at the door with an expectant look on his face.

"Anybody home?" Rich yelled, dropping his books on a chair and bending to retrieve the cat. He kicked the door shut and wandered through the living room, giving Logan a friendly scratch on the head. Normally, the cat was prone to ignore the coming and going of the human members of the family, unless, of course, he was hungry. Rich checked the food and water bowls in the kitchen. The water level was fine but, as he had suspected, the food bowl was empty. Rich filled it from a box of dry cat food, and Logan munched happily.

Grabbing an orange, Rich headed upstairs. He paused at his bedroom door to remove the tape seal, but it had already been torn away.

Wait a minute.

Rich stopped, immediately suspicious and annoyed. Fine. Somebody had decided to go into his room today. It was probably innocent; Mom had momentarily forgotten his paranoia and decided to leave something for him. He was bothered but tried to dismiss the worry. What could they find in there?

He shrugged and went inside. The harsh slap that caught him on the side of the head took him completely by surprise.

Rich dropped his orange. The motion tossed him down against the base of his dresser. He landed on a pile of magazines, hitting his back. The orange bounced and rolled against the far wall. "Just who do you think you are?" his father screamed.

Rich looked up from the floor. His face burned red, and he couldn't think.

Gus McFadden came out from behind the bedroom door. He was still in his green fatigue uniform, a work uniform with six wide stripes on both sleeves. He held a beer tightly in his left fist, and it had obviously not been his first. "Just who do you think you are to be protesting me?" he yelled.

"I didn't—"

His father kicked out with a viciousness that terrified Rich. The kick caught Rich in the stomach, knocking the air out of him, choking off his words.

"Don't lie to me!" yelled Gus. "You want to know who came to see me today? OSI! The OSI came to see me. Me, with twenty years of service in!"

Rich gasped, trying to recover his breath. He knew what the OSI was. The Air Force Office of Special Investigations. The undercover secret police branch that usually concentrated on busting servicemembers who used drugs. They were the only ones in the Air Force who never wore uniforms; they always operated in civilian clothes.

Gus took a gulp of his beer and spat. "You want to know what they asked me? They wanted to know what I knew about Stop the Nightmare. I said nothing. They said I should, since my son was hanging around with the top dogs of STN."

Rich tried to sit up. He managed this, despite the ache in his left side. He stared up at his father, who was now leaning on the cramped bookcase. Drinking and stewing. Rich didn't say anything. Why bother?

Gus shook his head. "Who are you to protest me?"

"I wasn't protesting you—"

"Shut up!" Gus tossed what was left of his beer at Rich, but he missed. The can zinged by and splattered the wall behind him, clinking to the floor. Gus shook his head again. "I don't begin to understand you. I taught you to fight, didn't I? To defend yourself? But you still come home bloody from school because you think it will all go away if you read enough." Gus paced the room, looking confused and disgusted. Finally he let out a cry of rage and yanked the entire bookcase down with a crash. Books scattered, and the old wooden frame bent and splintered.

"Why don't you protest that?" asked Gus.

Rich said nothing.

Everything collapsed. No matter how stable your life might seem, no matter how uneventful your days, you always lived in a house of cards. Ready to tumble with the coming of the wind.

Gus stood in the doorway, nodding now. "You want to know something else? I don't think you really believe in any of this anti-nuclear crap. I think maybe you just want to hurt your mom and me. Maybe you think we owe you something you're not getting."

Rich shuddered now. "You don't owe me anything."

Gus McFadden's face drew very cold. "That's right, kid. We don't owe you anything." He opened the closet, which had been trashed, and pulled a red suitcase out. He dropped it with a thump next to Rich and backed off. "There's your bag, kid, already packed. Get out of my house."

Rich looked at the suitcase and then at his father. "Dad, listen a minute—"

"I ain't your dad, kid," Gus cut in. "Get out."

Rich studied his father. He seemed more than serious and, worse, he seemed dangerous. At any moment he might become enraged again and start kicking. Rich managed to ask, "What about Mom?"

Gus shook his head. "She ain't your mom, either. How could she care about you after this? Mike is our only son."

Rich felt something swelling in his throat, and his eyes were growing hot. He was trying not to cry, but he was losing control and would have started if his father hadn't stopped the tears. "Why don't you crawl out of here on your knees? You look so comfortable down there," he snarled.

Rich choked it all back. He drew himself up and grabbed the suitcase. He was still wearing his jacket from school, so he lumbered into the hall and down the stairs without stopping. He could still hear his dad muttering in his room as he pushed his way through the front door.

Rich stood out on the front lawn and looked around, his mind reeling, trying to decide where to go. It was just four o'clock in the afternoon, and the sun was being battered away by the clouds. Old Sol hadn't made an honest showing all day. Rich consoled himself. If you don't like the weather in Montana, just wait five minutes. It will change.

Rich started down the street, dragging his suitcase and trying to make a joke out of the entire situation. The night of the big Homecoming dance and not only didn't he have a date, but he no longer even had a place to live. Yeah, that was just about right. Rich slowed his pace as he neared the corner, expecting Gus to step out onto the porch and call him back inside.

It didn't happen.

So much for parental remorse or fatherly regrets. Rich thought about the yellowing newspaper photo. The headline now read, SHARP MISSILE SERGEANT EVICTS WORTHLESS SON.

Rounding the corner, Rich continued walking. He knew he was wasting energy, but it was preferable to just thinking about it. He had absolutely no idea where he was going.

So was this how life as an adult began? Not as a medical student out to save the world but rather as a teenager dragging a suitcase around the neighborhood, trying to save himself? Rich knew the story, often repeated, of how Gus McFadden had left home at seventeen in order to enlist. Was that why Gus had tossed him into the street? Was this some sort of weird plan to straighten his son out? Back him into a corner where he would have no choice but to enlist?

Rich thought it over.

No way.

Stopping at the next corner, Rich sat down on the

suitcase. He was out of sight of the house now. Out of sight, out of mind. Wasn't that the line? Rich made a decision. He was not giving up Stop the Nightmare. It represented too much. STN was a whole new world beyond the harshness of school. The people there did not mock him when they spoke; they were friendly and interested. They asked questions:

"Hey, Rich, how's it going?"

"Rich, could you give me a hand with this?"

"Rich, do you want a soda?"

They were people who cared about something, and they acted as if they cared about him as well. More than that, they gave him a place to go where he didn't have to explain himself all the time. They offered escape. Escape from being Rich McFadden, the wimp. Rich McFadden, the geek with no friends. Rich McFadden, the bookworm who always got beat up after school. Rich McFadden, the clown with so many flip-outs behind him.

Rich had to sigh. He was alone on a street corner, with no answers in sight. He got up, grabbed the suitcase handle, and began walking again.

If keeping Stop the Nightmare in his life meant having to leave home, it was probably a fair exchange. More than a little frightening, perhaps, but he would manage it somehow. After all, was he not the same kid who sat in study hall solving all of the world's worst problems? Surely he could devise answers to a few of his own. Clear the path of all distractions, and the human mind was unstoppable.

Rich hesitated at the next corner, trying to choose a path. A route. A destination. He only hesitated a moment, though, and started off again, still uncertain. A little boy, no older than ten, rode by on a small bike. His eyes wide, he looked at Rich. What's the matter, kid, Rich wondered. Haven't you ever come across a member of America's homeless youth before?

When you were in trouble, Rich decided then, you went to your friends for help. But what did you do when you had no friends?

Find someone who doesn't hate you.

Rich walked a few more blocks and stopped in front

94

of a house. A thin cement walk snaked through a lawn, up to a two story frame house covered with white aluminum siding. The plaque on the mailbox read, CAPTAIN L.D. WESTPHAL AND FAMILY. There was no car in the driveway.

Jenny Westphal lived there.

Rich had still not figured out exactly who Jenny was, but she remained the only person who had ever said hello to him at school without a taunt in her voice. Rich also knew that she was as involved with STN as he was. Max would sometimes speak with admiration of the work she was doing for him. Rich guessed that she was skipping school to be there in the daytime, which had to be worse than just dropping by evenings. If nothing else, he probably owed it to her to warn her about what OSI was up to.

Would she listen? Or would she too laugh and call it another Rich McFadden flip-out?

Rich shuddered as he lugged his suitcase up the walk.

Twelve

Jenny wasted no time after school. Rushing home, she huddled herself in her room and confronted a mass of homework. Things seemed to be falling apart for her at school, even in algebra. While algebra had once been a friend, comforting her and giving good grades, it had suddenly turned and developed a nasty disposition. Jenny had missed too many classes. Over the course of the week she had skipped school twice entirely, and left midway through the day on Thursday. Today she had stuck it out but found herself hopelessly lost.

Surrounded by her books, Jenny couldn't help but be awed. The amount of material covered in two days was amazing. Two and a half chapters of sociology. An entire workbook section in natural science. She had a new song to learn for chorus, and missing three algebra classes had left her further back than she could as yet decipher. Even with study hall to play catch up, it was going to prove a nightmare. The biggest problem, of course, was resisting the urge to call Max.

Call Max? Why? What excuse would she use to call?

No excuse needed. She had stayed at school all day and just wanted to ask how things were going. She had to frown. So what are you now? His mother?

Jenny pulled the phone number from her purse and looked at it for a second, then set it aside. She brushed her hair back over her shoulders and bent over the textbook again. Hand me a snorkel; I'm diving in. That was when the knocking on the front door started. Jenny's first reaction was mild dread; she thought the Cockroach Woman had sent Kirk over to talk to her. Or maybe it was Patty, determined to save her from herself. The rapping continued. Against her better judgement, Jenny went downstairs to confront yet another complication in her life.

It was a different complication than the one Jenny had anticipated, though. What she found was Rich McFadden standing on the porch next to a red suitcase. This time there was no connection of Karma, or the circles binding the universe together. Or was there? Jenny was shocked, but she remembered telling Paul Lacey that she and Rich were going together. Was that why he was here with a suitcase? Had he heard? Did he expect to move in?

Crazy.

Jenny breathed out a deep breath. "Hi."

Rich nodded, not smiling. "My dad kicked me out of the house."

For a minute the statement made absolutely no sense to Jenny. Then her eyes widened. "What?"

"He kicked me out," said Rich. "Even packed my suitcase for me." He pointed at it.

Jenny looked from the suitcase back to Rich. She was confused. "How did that happen?" she asked.

Rich shrugged. "OSI told my dad I was working for STN."

Jenny had been an Air Force dependent long enough to know what OSI stood for. She looked up and down the street. Cloak and dagger stuff, she thought. "You better come in, I guess."

Rich followed her in, momentarily abandoning his case.

Jenny shook her head. "You better bring the bag."

Rich nodded, grabbing it. He didn't look comfortable, but Jenny couldn't find fault with that. Not after being tossed into the street. She shut the door. "Set the suitcase by the closet."

Rich did. He tucked his hands into his jacket pockets and looked around.

Jenny was playing the scene on instinct. She wouldn't

have known what to say otherwise. "Take off your coat," she said. "The house is well heated."

"Oh." Rich unzipped his jacket but hesitated to pull it off. He was still looking around.

"Something wrong?"

"I've never really been in a girl's house before."

Jenny thought that a strange thing to say, but she didn't know whether she should laugh or not. She decided not to. "Any difference?"

Rich finished looking around, then shook his head. "No."

Jenny nodded. "Come on. I'm working on more homework than the rest of the junior class combined." She started to lead him upstairs, but he wasn't following. She stopped and turned. "So what's wrong now?"

Rich made no response.

Jenny brushed her hair back over her shoulders and sighed. "Well, if you've never seen the inside of a girl's house, then you might be interested in seeing a girl's room. Strictly in the interest of science, right?"

Rich smiled. Almost. "Absolutely," he said.

"We can sort your troubles out while I sort out mine." Jenny turned and ran quickly upstairs, leaving Rich with no choice but to follow.

Rich appeared in the doorway, looking nervous, while Jenny dropped herself back among the books. She wanted to get serious about the algebra, but that was obviously a lost cause. Rich was looming there like a vulture.

Jenny picked up a pencil and played with it. She had to ask him. "How come you came over now?"

"What?"

"You never talked to me before."

Rich didn't say anything.

"I talked to you at the meeting, I say hi to you at school all the time, but you always space me off."

Rich hesitated. "I tried to call you once."

This really surprised Jenny. "You did?"

"Yeah, sort of."

"Sort of?"

"I did, yeah. You weren't home."

"Don't you believe in messages?"

"Messages?"

Jenny sighed. "I mean, you could have left a message. Right?"

"It was complicated."

"Life is complicated. I love it that way. Amuse me."

Rich frowned even more, if that was possible. And it was. "Your dad thought I was somebody else."

Jenny nodded. "That sounds about right. Did he think you were anybody I know?"

"I think so, yeah."

Jenny didn't ask anything else about it. She was treading into dangerous ground there. "Why did you call?"

"I don't know."

"What did you want?"

He shook his head.

"Maybe I shouldn't ask," Jenny said.

"Maybe not."

"So why are you so bold now?"

Rich shrugged. "Being homeless gives me a rugged, independent nature."

"You're not homeless."

"I know a very annoyed six foot two, one hundred ninety-nine-pound Master Sergeant who might tell you different."

Jenny exhaled again, the implications of Rich's plight just beginning to dawn on her. "So what are you going to do?"

Rich leaned against the doorframe. "I'm open to suggestions."

"Do you have enough money for a hotel?"

"That depends on how many minutes I have to stay there."

Jenny smiled. At least he still had a sense of humor. Jenny tried to picture herself in a similar situation but couldn't do it without seeing herself broken down and collapsed by now. Weeping, wandering, and losing time all over the place.

That was when she found the answer.

"Come on," she said, jumping off the bed and squeezing past Rich. She bounded down the stairs.

"What are we doing?" Rich was not far behind.

"We're making a call." Jenny grabbed the phone and turned to face him.

Rich drew back a bit. "Who are we calling?"

Jenny smiled now. "Max."

"You have his number?"

Jenny nodded. I am full of secrets, kid.

The connection went through, and the phone on the other end rang only once.

"Hello?" barked a voice. It was Max. He sounded ghastly.

Jenny had to hesitate. She reconsidered, wondering if it was really Max after all. Rich watched her with curious eyes. She pushed the telephone tight against her ear. "Max?"

He cleared his throat, but it didn't sound much better. "Yeah? Who else?"

"Are you all right?"

"Yeah. What do you think? Who is this?"

"It's Jenny."

There was a long pause, and then he cleared his throat once again. "Oh, yeah, Jenny. I'm sorry."

"What's wrong?"

"Nothing is wrong. What's up?"

She explained. Max listened without comment, and Jenny worried that he had hung up. He hadn't. He cursed finally, cleared his throat again, and said, "Okay, come over here."

"Thanks."

"Can you find the apartment if I give you the address?"

Jenny looked at Rich. He was leaning against the railing of the stairs, frowning. She nodded into the phone. "Yeah. I can find it."

Max read her the address and asked, "Do you need any kind of directions?"

"No. I know where that is."

"Okay. Come over." There was a click.

The line was disconnected.

100

Lost in her own thoughts, Jenny laid down the receiver. Rich looked expectant. "What happened?"

Jenny jerked herself back to reality. "Do you have any money at all?"

"Three weeks accumulated allowance."

"How much is that?"

"Almost twenty-two dollars. I have few expenses."

"Just as long as you have bus fare. We're going to see Max."

"At STN?"

"No." Jenny tried to smile, but her stomach was rolling. "We're going over to his apartment."

"You're coming with me?"

Jenny frowned. "Why? Did you want to go alone?"

Rich shook his head. "No, but I thought with OSI out there and all you might not want to—"

"I doubt you're being followed."

Rich looked embarrassed.

Jenny got a jacket and leg warmers from the closet. She didn't feel like changing shoes. Rich went to the piano and flipped through the sheet music while she got ready. "Do you play?" he asked.

Jenny shook her head. "The Cockroach—"

Rich glanced over.

"My stepmother," Jenny said.

"What?"

Jenny pulled on the second leg warmer. She looked away from Rich and said coldly, "My stepmother plays the piano."

Thirteen

"Come on inside."

Max backed up, ushering Rich and Jenny into his apartment, which was located just a few blocks from a bus stop in the Mall District. Rich was always amused by that. The Mall District in Greylake was little more than a cluster of apartment complexes opposite the shopping mall. Rich had been impressed with Jenny's sense of direction. She took them straight to the apartment. He was equally impressed with the apartment itself, which was on the ground floor of a vine-covered building and had its own patio. Max secured the door and followed them into the living room. He was wearing a grey suit jacket and trousers. A tie hung loosely around his unbuttoned shirt collar.

Max was unshaven and looked exhausted. His eyes were puffy red, but he dispelled any impression of sickness by speaking in a voice full of energy. He told Rich to set the suitcase down and asked them both to sit. Jenny eased down into a heavy chair across from the couch where Rich settled, suitcase off to the side. Max remained standing. "Tell it to me again," he said.

Rich took a breath and explained the attack by his father and the story about the OSI. While Rich talked, Max paced and nodded but didn't interrupt. Rich finally finished, saying, "Dad never really hit me before."

"He threw you out of the house?"

"He did."

Max nodded again and didn't speak. Finally he blew

out a breath and said, "I always figured they were watching us."

"Why would they watch us?"

"To stay one jump ahead. I wouldn't be surprised to find out they have somebody working with us, undercover."

Rich frowned. "But we're civilians. The Air Force doesn't have the authority to spy on us."

Max stopped and shrugged, and Rich immediately felt stupid.

Jenny was looking nervous now. "Are they going to tell my dad too?"

Max nodded. "Probably. If they figure out who you are."

That was what bothered Rich the most, and he said so. "How could they know who I am?"

"Valid question," said Max.

"Maybe they weren't really spying on you," Jenny cut in.

Max and Rich both looked at her.

Jenny tucked both feet under her in the chair and slipped her coat off and over the chairback. She explained what she meant. "We probably go to school with these OSI guys' kids," she said. "Maybe one of them knew you. Knows your dad or something."

Max looked at Rich now, making the entire thing a question to think about. Rich couldn't believe it was a case of chance recognition. He didn't know enough people; he didn't show his face around that many places. Or did he?

A question.

Max was speaking to Jenny. "I guess you better hang back for a while."

Jenny shook her head.

Max grew instantly annoyed. Or was he worried? "Jenny—"

"I'm committed."

"How committed will you be when your father, the capsule jock, comes down on you like a bag of bricks?"

Jenny didn't answer.

Max sighed. "I'm sorry." He turned and went down a hall of the apartment, disappearing into a room. Rich watched as Jenny rocked herself. Following her example, he unzipped his own jacket. It was hot in the apartment. He pulled it off, leaving it behind him on the couch.

Max reappeared in the living room, carrying a small suitcase of his own and an overnight bag. He set them by the door.

Jenny stopped rocking, her eyes wide again. "Are you going somewhere?"

"Yeah." Max walked back into the kitchen. "I have to go back to Michigan for a couple of days."

Jenny didn't seem to hear. "How long will you be gone?"

"A few days."

Max emerged from the kitchen with three canned sodas. He drank from one and handed the others to Rich and Jenny. Jenny thanked him, and Rich nodded. Max produced a set of keys. "You can stay here until this all blows over," he said to Rich. He extended the keys, shaking them with a jingle to get Rich's attention.

Rich made no move to accept. Until now the idea of actually staying somewhere other than his own room, insulated with its books, had been just fantasy. Even being tossed out by Gus had, in its own way, been unreal. Rich looked up at Max and said, "I . . . I don't want to get you in any trouble."

"What trouble?"

"If he freaks again. Decides he wants me back." Rich shrugged. "I'm not the glutton for punishment I once was."

Max shook his head. "We always talk about civil disobedience. Going to jail for the cause. That's all very well and good, but it's only so much brave talk if you turn away a friend in trouble just because he happens to be under eighteen."

Rich looked at Max. This was something new. "A friend?"

"Yeah. We're friends, aren't we?"

Rich nodded. "Yeah. I just don't want to start anything."

"I started this," said Max. "I asked you to come help me, and you did. You had courage. Take the keys."

Rich almost did, but then he stopped. He pictured himself wandering around in the strange apartment. He supposed that if he talked to Mom, he could probably go home. Despite what things might be like there. He grimaced to himself. So are you really a coward after all? You wrote all of those after school beatings off to your better nature, saying you wanted to change the world instead of just conforming to it. Was all of that just garbage?

Were you really a coward all along?

Max placed the keys directly into Rich's hand. "There's sheets in the bedroom closet. Food in the refrigerator. Just look around for whatever else you need." Max backed off, asking the last question in a kind voice. "What were you going to do, Rich? Sleep in the street?"

Max went to the front window. Was he worried about OSI, Rich wondered. No. Max had his bags packed, and he was ready to go. Back to Michigan, no doubt home for Thanksgiving.

Jenny asked, "Where's Baxter?"

Max didn't turn from the curtain. "Baxter's gone."

"Gone?" said Jenny. "Where?"

"I found him a better home."

"Why?"

Max looked at her now. "I can't keep a dog anymore."

"Why not?"

"I don't have time left for a dog."

Jenny paused just a beat. "Why are you going to Michigan?"

Rich was surprised. Jenny seemed obsessed with Max's leaving, annoyed that he might want to take a holiday trip to see his family and friends.

"I've got a few things to do," Max said. "Loose ends, you know."

Jenny nodded. "Who are you waiting for?"

"Karen."

105

"Is she your girlfriend?"

Max didn't exactly answer. "She's driving me to the airport."

"Will you be back before Thanksgiving?"

"Probably."

That blew one theory. It was already the twenty-second. Rich asked, "Aren't you going to spend it with your family?"

Max looked at them both. His smile was weak. "I thought you guys were my family."

Jenny took a long drink from her soda. Rich opened his now. It was an excuse not to say anything. A car door slammed outside and a knock at the door followed. Max answered. Karen from STN came chattering in, and she seemed surprised to see Jenny and Rich there. "Am I missing a meeting or something?" she asked.

Max told her what had happened to Rich. Her eyes got wide. "Oh, God, I'm sorry . . ."

Rich shrugged. "You didn't do it."

"What are you going to do?"

Max answered. "He's going to stay here."

Karen's eyes registered that information. Max went back down the hall for something, and Karen next smiled at Jenny. "Do I see you nights?"

Jenny shook her head. "I stuff envelopes. Some afternoons."

"Oh. What did you say your name was?"

"Jenny."

"Jenny what?"

She didn't get a chance to answer. Max came back and grabbed his bag, ushering her out the door ahead of him. "We're going to be late as it is." He paused on his way out to say one more thing to Rich and Jenny. "Keep out of things until I get back. Stay away from Stop the Nightmare."

Then he was gone.

Jenny stopped rocking. She took another drink of her soda. Rich watched her, wondering. Was she looking hurt because of Max's sudden exit or because he left with Karen?

Was there something between Jenny and Max that Rich didn't understand?

Rich abandoned his soda and looked at the small wind-up alarm clock on top of the television. It was nearly six. He glanced over at Jenny. "Aren't you going to Homecoming tonight?"

She shook her head. "No."

Rich was amazed. "You're kidding."

Jenny frowned. "Why should I be kidding?"

Rich was immediately embarrassed. It came out wrong again. "I just figured that you were going."

"Why? You're not going."

Rich laughed.

"Is that funny?"

"Many would think so."

Jenny was looking at the clock herself now. She announced the time out loud and sounded almost pleased with herself. "Six Oh-Two."

Rich lowered his eyes. "I'm sorry."

"What?"

"About your homework."

"I'll get to it."

Rich finally took note of Jenny's RAPID CITY SEE-GAR shirt. "Were you stationed at Ellsworth?"

Jenny nodded. "Three years."

"Long ago?"

"Junior high school."

"I was there until seventh grade."

Jenny nodded again. Then she totally nailed him by asking, "You want to go to a movie?"

Rich just looked at her.

"Is that a no?"

"No," said Rich. "I mean, what?"

"Stop playing games with me," she said impatiently. "Do you want to go to a movie?"

Rich shrugged. "Yeah."

"Good, we're progressing." She stood up. "Let's go."

Rich gaped at her again. "Just like that?"

"Why not? The theater is just across the street. Did you want to plan it out first?"

Rich shook his head.

"Then we're set." She started to pull her coat on. Watching her, Rich grew nervous. No, not nervous. Apprehensive. Not even that. Apprehensive was what he'd felt when he had approached her house that afternoon. Nervous was what he'd felt when he had knocked on her door.

Rich now felt shocked.

It boggled the mind.

Less than a day ago he had been the school geek. No friends, a quiet home life. Now his father had attacked him in an animal rage, throwing him into the street with one suitcase. It was a Friday night, and instead of wandering over to the library, Rich was staying in a strange apartment and was about to go to the movies with a very pretty girl from school.

"Don't forget your keys," said Jenny.

Rich pulled them off the suitcase and stuffed them into his pocket. He followed her out of the apartment, his mind reeling. It was absolutely amazing how much a little thing like nuclear war could change your whole life.

Fourteen

Jenny beat Rich to the ticket window of the theater. "One, please." She fumbled for her wallet. Rich was next in line and followed her into the theater lobby. An obnoxious usher was tearing tickets. Jenny couldn't help wondering why she was there. The best place for thinking was home. That didn't feel right, though. Rich had too many problems of his own, and it wouldn't be fair to abandon him. Would it?

Probably not. But why are you really here?

I don't want to be abandoned either. Satisfied?

Almost.

"Want some popcorn?" Rich was beside her now.

Jenny grimaced. "My stomach's too weird right now."

"Sure?" He looked concerned.

Jenny nodded. Routine. The same conversation had occured on every movie date Jenny had. But was this a date? Probably not. Okay, maybe, but no big deal. Movies were safe. They killed time, required no brilliant conversation, and gave you something to talk about afterwards. Neat little invention, films. Helped you avoid the really "big" subjects, like whatever it was that had brought you together with the guy in the first place.

Normally the answer to that was simple. History class, a chance introduction at a party, mutual friends. But school was freaky these days, Jenny didn't go to many parties anymore, and her friends were becoming distant. So what brought her together with Rich?

The nuclear disarmament movement.

109

Exactly how weird was life going to get?

Rich stood near a cardboard display of an upcoming feature, looking very nervous. COMING FOR CHRISTMAS! read the display. The feature was called *The Last American Soldier*, and the poster showed a muscular guy cradling a heavy machine gun in his arms, an ammunition belt slung over his shoulder. Jenny walked up beside Rich. "How does the movie look?"

Rich shrugged. "Another warmonger decides to solve the world's problems with armor-piercing bullets."

Jenny smiled because she felt she owed it to him. Rich seemed absolutely terrified. Rattled. There was something about the popcorn turn-down that usually reduced a movie date to rubble, but she thought Rich might be different. After all, he had other things to worry about. There was something about not letting a guy buy you anything that seemed to destroy him inside. And Rich didn't need any more aggravation.

Jenny had to sigh.

Okay, why not?

She asked, "Is the popcorn offer still open?"

"What?" Rich almost jerked. Jenny felt sure that if she reached for him, he would panic and leap away through the nearest door or window. She told him that if he still felt like getting some popcorn, she was up to it. "But only with extra butter."

Rich smiled, rushing off to the counter.

And so the madness begins again.

Maybe not, Jenny thought. All I have to do is maintain an element of control. Not like with Kirk.

So is this a real date?

Not yet.

Not if I can help it.

So Jenny sat in the dark theater alone, in the seat next to Rich. The film was a science fiction thing called *The Greenhouse Effect*. It was sort of about the end of the world, except that it had nothing to do with nuclear weapons. There had been a plague, and everyone in the world—with the exception of the film's hero—was infected with

110

a germ which was harmless except for the fact that it produced LSD in the bloodstream.

Everyone in the world was stoned on acid.

Jenny sat passively, watching the movie, letting it happen. Things got more and more bizarre on the screen, but at least she didn't have to talk to Rich. At least she didn't have to deal with that situation. The dialogue on screen was bad, but the lines running through her head were worse.

What can I do?

What about me? What about him?

What can he do?

Why am I here?

That was always the question lately, wasn't it?

Why am I here?

Where did Max go?

Michigan? So he said. But where did he *really* go?

The movie played over her, like a dream. Which was strange, but at the same time real. Real, because in her dreams of late Jenny was always watching a movie. The film *First Strike*. In her dreams everyone was there watching, and the missile launch officer depicted on screen no longer simply resembled her father, as the man in the first film had. Lately, the officer *was* her father, Captain Daddy himself, the guy with the greying brown hair and the thick white surgical scar on his lower lip. Sometimes the scar seemed so big that it took up the entire screen.

Captain Daddy, up there in the movie. Captain Daddy, looking quite trim and proper in his dark blue United States Air Force jumpsuit with the colorful patches on the shoulders.

And this time it all seemed real.

No longer was it just a movie being shown for some kids with signed parental permission slips. Somewhere over the North Pole World War Three had begun, and now it came down to this.

Captain Daddy, moving so slowly, turning to the other officer who shared his grim task. Handing him a short silver chain with a key attached. The light caught the key, and it glistened. Jenny could see that the other officer was

111

Tripper. Tripper looked out at Jenny and smiled an embarrassed little smile.

Separated by twenty feet of computer console, both officers in the small launch capsule inserted their keys into special locks. Captain Daddy chanted, "One, two, three—rotate!"

Keys turned.

"Sequence armed," said Tripper. "I have a good authentication from SAC."

Captain Daddy nodded. Always nodded. "Fire control safety switches to the manual 'Off' position."

"Roger that. Checklist nine complete."

Maxwell Neuger stood up suddenly in the audience. He was screaming, his voice pained. He didn't seem well. The noise he made was bloodcurdling and shrill. He was screaming, "No, Jenny, no!"

Jenny looked out across the audience. She saw Maxwell Neuger; he was between Reverend Lowell and Rich. She had to blink it back. Marcie was there as well, which was strange and wrong, because Marcie didn't have a permission slip. Maybe she did now. Maybe she had conned her father into signing it. Patty was standing near her, and Jenny hoped Patty would be able to keep Marcie straight. Sometimes she was so gullible. Kirk was out there too, painting. What was he painting?

One breath.

Another.

It was very cold in the launch capsule. The silver chain which hung from the key in her hand was Jenny's silver birthday necklace. The key was in its special lock. A voice was shouting.

"Display arming lights—on!"

Captain Daddy nodded into a red telephone. "Stand by all stations for green missile away lights. I have a confirmed all flight enable, a confirmed station enable."

He turned to Jenny. He was not the Captain anymore; he was Lance Westphal, her father. He seemed so very sad, sadder even than after Jenny's mother left. He seemed to reach inside and find strength, though. He touched

Jenny lightly on the arm. "We have just one more thing to do."

Jenny blinked. Heart pounding.

Maxwell Neuger still yelled, still pleaded. But he could never get to Jenny, not in her dream. In her dream she was in the movie.

Was it a movie? Or was it supposed to be real?

Her father looked at her closely and for one moment transformed into the Captain again, frightening Jenny. "Baby? You're my best girl, right? And who am I?"

She mouthed the words 'Captain Daddy,' but there was no sound.

He seemed to understand anyway and nodded. Captain Daddy had never seemed so compassionate. His eyes seemed almost to twinkle as his brow furrowed. They were blazing eyes. They were Maxwell Neuger's eyes. "Jenny, it's just you and me now. Mommy's gone. I'm sorry. It's just you and me. No doctors at all. I need you to activate the firing sequence. That is all. Then the missiles will launch and it will all be over. Can you do that? Please? The switches are right here. Go ahead and push them."

Jenny paused.

She could not decide.

There was something in the dream that could always be different. Sometimes it came to her, and sometimes it didn't. Later, she could never recall what it was, exactly. Only that it was something her mother had told her, years before.

"Jenny, there isn't much time. You have to push the firing switches now. Jenny, please!"

Captain Daddy's voice seemed so much firmer now.

In the audience, Jenny could hear them. Some were begging, pleading no. Others were yelling for her to find the courage to do it. Many were deathly quiet. They were only waiting for her to decide.

Soon the hush whispered like a wind, and everyone was quiet.

Everyone waited.

Jenny's hand hovered over the ten black switches,

which were after all not so very much different from any wall light switch.

She ignored Captain Daddy. She ignored the silence of everyone watching her in the movie. Then she saw the razor in the bathtub and heard the one voice that pushed her to switch off the lights and make the world go away. The voice of the Cockroach Woman saying, "*I didn't think she could do it. Even her own mother didn't want her.*"

"Jenny?"

Jenny recoiled. It was like the worst of her days before Doctor Pipps. She went from being immersed in the movie to walking with Rich in the parking lot of the mall. It would be zombie time if she let that continue.

"You look spooked."

Jenny shrugged it off. "Weird movie."

"Yeah."

It was almost nine-thirty; the parking lot lamps glowed overhead as they walked between rows of cars. There was a McDonald's across the lot, and when Rich asked if she was hungry, she nodded without thinking. That wasn't true. She was thinking, but she was thinking about Mom. Which was definitely a bad sign. Whenever she started thinking about Mom, she started seeing razors in the bathtub, and she started losing time all over the place. And Doctor Pipps was too far away to help.

Rich stopped walking. Jenny waited, but he said, "I think I know."

"What?"

"You're afraid to be seen with me."

Jenny looked at him, a bit boggled by that. "What?"

"It's Homecoming night, and I appreciate your helping me, but I think I know why you don't want to be seen with me."

"Why is that?"

"Well." Rich seemed to have to dredge it out. "I'm a geek."

Jenny looked at him. At his bright face, his glasses, the smile that showed too rarely. Why did she care? Was he a geek? Now that she thought about it, the answer was

114

no. She said, "When you start acting like a geek, I'll let you know."

Rich seemed surprised by this. "Really?"

"It's a promise."

So they went to McDonald's after all.

Sitting opposite each other in a booth, they ate, and Jenny asked, "Okay, so what else is bothering you?"

Rich nibbled a french fry. "You want the list?"

"I don't know. How long is it?"

"Extensive. How about yours?"

Jenny thought about it. "Such a list would boggle the mind."

"Okay. So what is item number one?"

Jenny thought about it again, then said simply, "Ice cream, I think."

"Ice cream?"

"Yeah. It doesn't have any bones. Ever think about that? Ever wonder what an ice cream skeleton would look like?"

Rich laughed. "No."

"I have. I think it would be a gruesome thing to see."

They both laughed. "Okay. What's your number one?" Jenny asked.

"I can't tell you."

"Why not?"

"We'd be here all night."

"Okay," said Jenny. "I've got nowhere else to go."

Rich seemed to think about that. He said, "That's not true. You've got friends all over. People . . ."

People? Jenny looked at Rich, trying to see into his eyes. What sort of eyes were they? Clear and blue, but what exactly were they hiding? "What do you mean, people?"

"Uh . . . guys." He looked away.

"Oh." Jenny saw what he was saying. She nodded. "Well, it's possible to have *people* waiting for you all over and still feel all alone."

Rich seemed shocked by this. "I always figured that was all I wanted out of life."

"What? A girlfriend?"

115

He was definitely embarrassed now. "Yeah . . ."

"So what if you had a girlfriend? Where would she be now? Would she be here with you now?"

"I don't know."

"There you go," said Jenny. "That's exactly what I'm talking about. You can never tell about people. Ever."

"What about you?"

"Me?" Jenny took a drink of her soda. "What if I was your girlfriend?"

Rich seemed unable to breathe. He nodded. "Yeah."

Am I egging him on, Jenny wondered. "I'm undependable," she said. "You wouldn't like me. And I'm changing."

"What do you mean, changing?"

"I become less dependable every day."

Rich swallowed. He seemed to be working up to say something. Jenny cut him off, asking again, "Tell me. What's number one on your troubles list?"

Rich shook his head. "No. I'll give you number one sixty-two."

"Number what?"

"One sixty-two."

Jenny blew out some air. "Hey, how long is your list?"

"Endless."

"You said extensive."

"I lose track. Life's a bitch, and then you die."

Jenny nodded. "Maybe so, but it can't be soon enough for me." They both stopped laughing.

Rich nodded a bit too, taking time to sip his soda. "I used to say that. Think that."

"What?"

"That I was ready to die."

Jenny watched him closely. "And are you still?"

"Ready to die?"

"Yeah."

"Not really."

Jenny nodded again and finished her french fries.

"What about you?" asked Rich. "Are you ready to die?"

Jenny shrugged. "Sometimes. Yeah."

"Why?"

"What's number one sixty-two?"

Rich thought about it. "Really want to know?"

"Yeah."

"Seventh grade. Valentine's Day. Remember?"

"What about it?" Jenny didn't follow the thought.

"I was in Homeroom when they came in with the flowers. The red carnations that the cheerleaders were selling. Remember now?"

Jenny shrugged. "They do that every year."

"Yeah, but when I was in seventh grade, they gave me a flower."

"Oh, yeah?"

"Yeah, and you're wondering: so what? I never got a flower before, and never since. Who wants to send me one? But there I was in seventh grade Homeroom, and this cheerleader smiles at me. Dawn Russell. Know her?"

"Yeah."

"Dawn Russell smiled at me and handed me a flower. Said, 'Happy Valentine's Day.'"

Jenny felt her stomach knot up a bit. Here it comes. Rich wasn't talking anymore, so she had to say, "And?"

He shrugged. "Big joke. Big mistake. I hold this flower about five minutes, all excited and wondering who might have sent it, and Dawn starts giggling. 'Oh, I made a mistake,' she says. Flower was supposed to go to Rob McCallen, who thanks to the alphabet sat three rows back. She snatches the flower from me, still laughing, and gives it to him. Everybody laughed."

Rich went on. "But have you ever had one of those moments? One of those moments when, just for a few seconds, you think the world might be all right after all? That maybe it's not a cheat? That maybe there's just a little bit for everyone?"

Rich stopped talking. Jenny watched him. He was wadding up his wrappers, sticking them into the paper bag the food came in. He looked up again. "That's what I consider number one sixty-two."

Fifteen

Embarrassed, Rich waited for Jenny's reaction. The story had just sort of popped out; it wasn't what he'd meant to say and obviously the openness bothered Jenny. Terrific. He was losing her. Rich crushed the debris-filled food bag into a small ball.

What was it Jenny said to him that first night at the Stop the Nightmare meeting? Something about needing to talk to him? Was this the talk, finally? Why?

Jenny was looking very seriously at her plastic cup and straw. Maybe she was still with him, but maybe she was really miles away.

Who was she?

Jenny finally shrugged. "We all make lists, we all have problems. Some are pretend, some are for real."

"Which are worse?"

Jenny didn't answer.

Rich thought a second before asking, "Are you really ready to die?"

"Who said I was ready?"

"You did."

"Okay. So what if I am?" Jenny pushed her tray away. "Obviously, most people are ready to die."

"Why?"

"Look at Stop the Nightmare. Out of all the people in Montana—in the whole country—how many really care one way or another about the nuclear thing?"

Rich shrugged. "Not many."

"And what about you?"

"Me?" He wanted to get the words, the thoughts right. But instead, he just said what he was thinking. "I don't care that much about dying. Everybody dies. But I don't want everybody to die at once. That's a nightmare. The sun rising one morning, and all the people are gone. That's what it means to me."

"Yeah. But how far will you go to fight it?"

Rich didn't know how to answer that.

Jenny said, "I think there's only one person around here who wants to live bad enough to really do anything about it. That's Max."

Max? For a split second Rich felt . . . What? Jealous? That was crazy. Max was someone with important things ahead of him. It was only right that Jenny should admire him. Still . . . Rich felt he should defend himself. She saw Max as important. Rich wanted to be seen as important too. He said, "I did get kicked out of my house for STN."

"For STN? Is that all?"

"I won't be going back."

"No?"

Rich emphasized it. "No."

Jenny brushed her hair back. "Well, we can talk all we want, but we need to start doing things."

"Like what?"

"Max will know."

Rich nodded, unsure—no, not even remotely aware—of what to say next. "You know," he tried, "it says in the Bible that someday the lambs *will* lie down with the lions."

"Yeah?" said Jenny. "That might work. Just as long as you keep a fresh supply of lambs on hand."

Rich swallowed. He wanted to keep a hand in the conversation, but he was still numbed about even sitting there with Jenny. He couldn't say it aloud, but Dad, the eviction, STN and OSI were really nothing in comparison. This was the big event. He wanted to make it last, which it wouldn't do if he said the wrong thing.

Jenny was staring over his shoulder, saying nothing.

Rich prodded a little. "So why do you feel like dying?"

"Why?"

"Yeah."

"Maybe because I feel like I'm already dying. One small piece at a time."

Rich thought about that. He thought about what it felt like to stand before a bunch of kids, defenseless and bloody. It felt like dying. Dying one small piece at a time. "You saw me get beat up," he said.

"Yeah."

"Did you wonder why I never fight back?"

"Yeah," Jenny responded. "But I wasn't going to ask."

"How do you feel about being a dependent?"

"What?"

"How do you feel about being an Air Force dependent? Do you think about it?"

"Yeah. I don't like it."

Rich nodded. That was easy. How could he explain the next? "My dad takes everything casually. Like this is the way things are supposed to be, forget about ever changing anything. He works on nuclear weapons, but he doesn't call them that. He calls them nukes. Nothing important, right? Just workin' on some nukes. He never thinks about what they are, or what they can do."

Rich took a breath. "Everything is military to him; everything is Air Force. Which is funny, since he isn't even important. He's just a Master Sergeant, just a flunkie working on nukes. Just a guy making sure that when the time comes, millions of people will die as planned."

Jenny seemed confused. "And that's why you don't fight?"

"No, wait a minute." Rich bit his lip. "I always go off like this, and I never make any sense. Rich McFadden flip-out. Right?" He tried to clear his mind, keep his thoughts in order. "I don't fight because there shouldn't be any fighting. Everybody says that—pacifism, world peace. Right. Peace, just so long as the other guy stops fighting first. That's crazy. Everybody wants to stop fighting, but nobody wants to be the *first* to stop fighting. Well." Rich looked Jenny in the eye. "I don't mind being the first to stop fighting."

Jenny met his eyes, and Rich liked that. He liked looking into her eyes, trying to see into them. Jenny said, "Not fighting should be enough. You shouldn't have to need any reasons."

Rich smiled, but it felt weak. "Yeah, but I guess an excuse helps you sleep at night."

"I don't sleep much."

Rich had to nod. "Yeah. Me neither."

Jenny didn't say anything for a minute, and then she sighed. "I hate my mother. Isn't that typical?"

"Your stepmother?"

Jenny shook her head. "My stepmother I merely dislike. Abject hatred is reserved for the woman who gave birth to me."

"Why?"

"You really like to compile these lists, don't you?"

Rich didn't answer. He was looking over Jenny's shoulder. Two girls had pulled away from their guys and were walking over. The game was obviously over; there were lines at the counter, and the outside lot was filling with cars.

The first girl, a straight-haired blonde, reached the booth. She glanced at Rich and rolled her eyes. Then she looked at Jenny and said, "Kirk was looking for you."

Kirk, thought Rich. He sank deeper into the booth.

Jenny smirked. "Say hello, Patty."

The blonde girl turned to Rich again. Her smile seemed fake. Or was he paranoid? "Hi."

Rich tried to grunt a reply, but not much came out.

The other girl, a frizzy redhead, giggled. "Hi, I'm Marcie."

Rich got his throat clear. "Hi. Hello."

Patty was still talking to Jenny. "Kirk wants to know if you're going to help out with the school play."

"Yeah," said Marcie. "You should. I am."

"What is it?"

"A musical. *Oklahoma!*"

Jenny shook her head. "I don't sing solo. I need to be lost in a crowd."

Patty smirked again. "You don't have to sing. The

play's already cast. He's looking for people to help out backstage."

Marcie laughed. "I'm painting sets."

"I think it's absolutely essential that you get involved with something," Patty said.

"Or someone?"

"Maybe. That depends."

Depends, thought Rich, feeling like a puppy with his nose pressed against the glass. Depends on who, who being anyone but Rich McFadden, no doubt.

"I've got something to be involved with," Jenny said.

"What?"

"STN."

"Don't be stupid."

"Stupid?" Jenny sat up in the booth. She seemed angry. "You think it's stupid?"

Patty sighed. "No. I just think it's pointless. Why are you wasting yourself on that stuff?"

"What do you mean, wasting myself?"

"This is your junior year."

"There may not *be* a senior year. Have you ever thought about that?"

Now Patty definitely rolled her eyes.

Marcie, the redhead, jumped in to change the subject. She smiled at Rich and asked, "Are you guys going to Diane's party?"

Patty looked at Rich, waiting.

On the spot, Rich looked at Jenny, waiting.

Jenny still seemed angry. She shook her head. "No."

Patty frowned at that. She said, "You quit RT, didn't you?"

Jenny looked up. It was her turn to look confused. "I just missed a couple of meetings. Who told you that?"

Now Marcie backed off and looked away.

Patty continued, "I didn't see you guys at the game."

"No."

"So why didn't you call me? I thought we were all going to work this one out together?"

"I've been busy. Sorry," Jenny mumbled.

"All week?"

"Not all week. I just didn't want to go to Homecoming. Okay?"

"You might have told us."

Marcie nodded in agreement.

Patty looked over towards the counter, where some guys were waiting with food. "We gotta go," she said. She gave Jenny a weird look and bounced off.

"Be careful," Marcie warned before she left as well.

Rich looked across the booth. He felt as crumpled as the cup and straw Jenny was playing with. "You want another?" he asked.

"No. I want to leave now."

Rich followed her out. A battered green Chevy jerked to a halt in the parking drive directly in front of them. A guy stuck his head out of the passenger window. He seemed tall and skinny and wild. He yelled, pointing. "Jenny! Hey, Jenny!"

Rich looked at her. She closed her eyes a second.

The guy in the car asked, "Is that him? Are you serious?"

Once again, Jenny seemed ready to boil over. "I'm always serious!"

"And that's the guy?"

"Find somebody who cares, Paul!"

The guy driving the car laughed, and the tall one leaning out the window shook his head. "Kirk's looking for you."

"I'm easy to find."

"I asked him about everything."

"Great. Did you two have a good time discussing my life?"

The guy started to say something else, but another car was behind them and blew its horn. The Chevy jerked forward, around to the drive-thru window.

Jenny seemed more than a little annoyed.

Rich looked at her. "What guy am I supposed to be?"

Jenny shook her head. "If you ask that question, you'll never have a chance with me." She took off across the lot.

Rich stood there a moment, feeling as though he had

been kicked in the chest. Never have a chance with her? He never expected to have a chance with her. His blood was racing, but it still took a courageous effort to follow.

When he caught up with her, Jenny started talking as if none of the evening had happened. "So what are you going to do? Are you going to go home?"

"Who was that guy back there? In the car?"

Jenny looked at him hard. "So much for ever having me love you."

Rich lost a breath. "What?"

"There doesn't always have to be a reason, you know. Questions don't have to be asked to be answered."

Jenny ran away from him, towards a lone car parked beneath a lighted lamp post. "Do you know what this is?" she asked. Rich caught up again and shook his head. "It's a likely car." She began to jump about, doing a variation of the Mexican Hat Dance around the car. She sang aloud as she did it, "Da da, da da, da dump . . ."

Rich just watched. "A likely car?"

"Likely cars are so rare and difficult to find. They're like friends who ask only the right questions." Jenny had stopped, and now she looked to the sky. "I wish it were raining. God, I wish it were raining. I want to dance in the rain."

Rich stared at her. By now he was hopelessly confused.

"What are you going to do?" Jenny repeated. "Go home?"

"No. Dad's probably still drinking anyway."

"Does he drink a lot?"

"Does it matter?"

"I guess it might." Jenny seemed to be wilting a bit.

"I don't like to use that as a crutch. You know? I act the way I do because my dad drinks beer. That's stupid."

They started walking across the lot again. After a few minutes passed, in which they seemed to got no closer to the road, Jenny said, "Do you know what the ultimate suicide note would be?" She spread her hands out parallel to the ground, lifting her palms up to the sky. "The ultimate suicide note would be a long, very long poem.

A warm goodbye kiss to the world. Do you ever read poems?"

"No."

"Maybe you should."

"Are they all as scary as you?"

"I'm not scary. Just cold and weird." Jenny started walking again. They were reaching the road. "All traits I picked up from the Cockroach Woman."

"The who?"

"Nobody."

"You said that before. Who's the Cockroach Woman?"

Jenny seemed to take an extra breath. "That's my step-mother. Like I said, I don't treat her so good."

"Does she deserve it?"

"I used to think so."

"And now?"

"Now? Who can say?"

Rich nodded. They were across the street now, nearing the bus stop where, hours before, he and Jenny had climbed down from the bus to see Max. Rich was trying to make the evening last, trying to stop Jenny from leaving, so he pushed a little. "So what happened to your mom? Did she leave?"

Jenny shrugged. "Yeah, I guess."

"You guess."

"I guess she did, but it's hard to explain."

"Yeah," said Rich. So much for that.

"She loved to dance in the rain."

"Like you wanted to."

Jenny shook her head. "I wanted to. She did."

Rich thought a second. "How long ago . . . ?"

"My mother left me when we were in Rapid City. Okay? My dad was in the missile field at Ellsworth, and one day she wasn't there anymore. No big deal, really. Is it?"

Rich didn't know what to say.

Jenny just smiled. "Sorry. This is one of the few topics on which I cannot babble incoherently for hours."

"Oh. You talk a lot?"

"I used to."

"You used to?"

"I used to do a lot of things. I don't talk so much anymore. Not until tonight, anyway."

"Why not?"

"I guess I just ran out of things to say."

"Oh. Welcome to the club."

Jenny hesitated. "I write things down sometimes."

"Really?"

She nodded. "Yeah. In notes. To myself."

"Does it ever scare you that maybe somebody will read the notes?"

"No, it happened. I survived. Pretty much."

"How did it feel?"

"Sick." Jenny continued, her voice flat. "I don't feel so much any more. It's easier."

Rich felt abandoned, then chilled. The Greylake CityBus slid into the stop, airbrakes hissing. The door popped open, driver waiting.

Rich groped for the words. "Hey. Maybe we could do this again. Just talk . . ."

"No," Jenny said.

"What?"

"We've got enough problems, with STN and everything. We don't need each other on top of that."

"But why not?" Rich asked.

Jenny answered as the driver reached to close the door. "I don't want to be on that list of things bothering you."

You already are, Rich wanted to tell her. But the doors were closed and the bus hissed, pulling away.

Sixteen

In the days just prior to Thanksgiving break, Jenny managed to drop even further behind in school. The reasons were almost totally beyond her control.

Her original plan had been to go back to school and salvage what she could. Catch up on her class work and accept seriously Max's warning to stay away from the Stop the Nightmare office. She hadn't talked to Rich since Friday night, and she spent most of the weekend buttoned up in her room, struggling with the accumulated homework.

Monday Rich wasn't at school.

He wasn't there on Tuesday either.

By Wednesday, Jenny was a wreck with worry. Worry? Why?

Because he is a person, she thought.

Sociology was Jenny's first class of the day, and she had grown used to passing Rich at his locker on her way in. After repeated calls to Max's apartment, with no answer, Jenny decided to leave school early on Wednesday.

She felt sick about skipping school again. There would be trouble, eventually. It had to happen. She departed the base by bus, heading first to the apartment. She had no idea what she was going to say when she got there.

Snow had started to fall on Saturday night and had been continuing on and off since then. The Mall District was kept well plowed, though, and all Jenny had to deal with when she stepped down from the bus was wet, salted pavement. Blowing out a foggy breath, she went quickly to the apartment. It was locked, and nobody answered the doorbell.

Jenny stood on the steps for a few moments. There was really no way for her to determine whether anyone was there or not. Was Rich really gone, or was he upset? Had what she said been so bad? Or was there a real problem, one she didn't understand?

Against her better judgement, Jenny decided to check with the Stop the Nightmare office. She went to the Mall for change from her last five dollar bill and then stepped back out to await the crosstown bus. It was almost two o'clock before she arrived on Eighth Street.

Karen was the only one working in the STN office. Jenny hesitated at the doorway. Karen raised her head at the opening door and covered an initial frown with a fast smile. "Hi, Jenny, how are you?"

Jenny closed the door behind her. She nodded.

"Did you stop by to stuff some more envelopes?" Karen asked brightly. "If you did, it's not really necessary. We're finished with the initial mailings."

"I'm looking for Rich."

"He's not here."

"What about Max?"

Karen obviously did her best to maintain her smile, but it slipped a bit. "I'm sorry; he's not around."

"Is he still in Michigan?"

"I couldn't tell you."

"Who could?"

The smile wavered more. "Why are you so concerned?"

"He was sick."

"Right."

Jenny blinked back. She didn't understand the weird signals she was getting from Karen, but she found them definitely negative. Maybe hostile. "What about Reverend Lowell? Would he know anything?"

"If you're smart, you won't bother."

Jenny's jaw dropped. This woman was really getting nasty.

Karen shook her head. "The way things seem, it just

might be best if Maxwell Neuger stays away from STN for a while."

"What do you mean?"

Karen didn't sound happy at all. "He and his pal Milo have managed to mess up just about everything Reverend Lowell got going. I told him so, too."

"Would you tell me what's going on?" Jenny pleaded. "Please."

Karen pulled a pack of cigarettes from her desk drawer and lit one. "What's your question?"

Jenny hesitated, then decided to ask the obvious. "Were you going with him?"

Karen waited a moment, trying to watch Jenny's eyes, it seemed, then she shook her head. "No. Maybe I even wanted to. He was cute; he was nice. But we never did anything steady."

"Why not?"

"He's unreliable."

"How?"

"He borrowed my car once and disappeared for a week. Can you believe that? I was late for work four times. He's a maniac. And he's a liar."

A chill raced the length of Jenny's spine.

Those eyes.

Karen snorted. "To think that all that time I thought he was sick."

"What?"

"All that time he was dragging himself around, tired and sick to his stomach. Throwing up in my bathroom. He wasn't sick. I was at his house once; it's full of drugs. I even think he uses a needle."

Jenny felt chilled again.

She had abandoned Rich there.

And now he was gone.

What had happened to him? Was Max responsible?

Karen looked up, meeting Jenny's eyes. She frowned. "I'm thinking about quitting STN."

Jenny blinked. "You are?"

"There's a lot of bad stuff coming down. Take it from me. You don't want to be here when it happens."

Jenny nodded. She was beginning to wonder the same thing: Did she really need to be around all of this? Probably not. There was one thing she needed, though, and she said it. "I need to talk to them."

"Them?"

"Rich and Max."

"Is there a problem?"

"It's my problem."

Karen took a final drag of her cigarette. "Okay. But aren't you a little young to be chasing after junkies?"

Jenny left the office, confused about where to go next.

She went looking for Reverend Lowell, and found him an hour and a half later. Reverend Mark Lowell kept his office in the rear of the First Fellowship Church of Greylake. She knocked and heard a voice call, "Enter!" She did. The office was full of fish. She blinked it back, thinking it a dream, or a nightmare, of her own lost red bettas. Three expensive aquariums lined the walls, including a one hundred ten-gallon tank. Jenny paused, awed.

Reverend Lowell jumped up, proud of his display. He gestured to a group of large silver fish in the middle tank. "Jack Dempsey fish. Named after the famous boxer."

Jenny recognized them. "I used to keep fish myself."

"Used to? Grab a seat." Reverend Lowell watched her sit before settling back into his own chair. "What made you lose interest?"

"The fish lost interest."

"What?"

"They died."

Reverend Lowell watched her a moment. "I'm sorry."

"So were they," said Jenny. Then she added, "I need to know how to get in touch with Max."

Reverend Lowell tightened his gaze. "Is there some sort of problem?"

"Should there be?"

"I just wondered if I could help."

Jenny fought the sudden hurting and nervesickness that was creeping over her. She wondered what Reverend Lowell was hiding, but his eyes revealed nothing. She said, "Everybody seems to think Max is up to something bad. Is he?"

Reverend Lowell shook his head slowly. "No. But there are some . . . difficulties."

"Drugs?" she blurted out.

"I really can't discuss that."

"He's my friend, too."

Reverend Lowell nodded. "Then of course you understand."

Jenny shivered. "It isn't just that. I'm worried about Rich . . ."

"You mean about his problems at home?"

"Yeah."

"I know about those."

"Well, can't anyone help?"

"I've tried talking to his father. It's a very uneasy situation. If necessary, I can talk to Sergeant McFadden's commander at the base . . ."

"What?" That was incredible. The anti-nuclear Reverend was talking about calling Rich's dad's commander.

"Be patient, Jenny," Reverend Lowell said. "God corrects things in his own time."

"God isn't enough," she said. "I think we need some help."

Reverend Lowell looked into her eyes now. He seemed tired. "Maybe not. Maybe sometimes He isn't enough. But what else is there?"

"There used to be friends," said Jenny, but she knew that was no longer true. Max had been her friend, and what had he proven to be? Just another druggie. Pretending to believe in an important cause. Was that a thrill for him, like the drugs? Probably. Max had lied about being a friend, just as Jenny had, intentionally or not, lied to Patty and Marcie about being their friend. And Rich. Where did he fit into this? As the victim, as always. Jenny's eyes were stinging, so she turned away. She decided not to believe in anything anymore. And having made that decision, she decided to go home. She wanted to discover which version of the lie was being told there.

Seventeen

Max had returned to Greylake, arriving back in town the previous Monday morning, slipping into the apartment after midnight with a duplicate set of keys. He had been gone only two days. Rich awakened on the couch and saw Max in the chair across from him. Rich had fallen asleep soothed by the low buzz of the television, and now, bathed in the set's snowy glow, Max seemed very pale. His eyes were fixed on some invisible point on the ceiling. His beard was thicker, and he seemed rumpled and wrinkled sitting there in the same grey suit he'd worn when he had left. His necktie was knotted and tied around his left fist.

Rich sat up, pushing away the blanket he was hiding under. The wind-up alarm clock on the television indicated three-seventeen. Rich sniffed and scratched his head.

Max said nothing.

Rich felt the need to apologize. For being there. For intruding into a private life. Like a Peeping Tom astride a garbage can, he realized that, regardless of what you saw through the window, it had been wrong to look in the first place. Rich felt like crawling away somewhere. "I had some money," he said. There was no reply. Rich cleared his throat and explained. "I replaced the sodas. Saturday I ate out, but today I had some corn flakes."

Max coughed, never moving his eyes from the spot on the ceiling. "Whatever you did was right."

"It was really warm so I turned the heat down."

"Fine."

"Is it too low for you?"

"It's okay."

Rich nodded. The television continued its snowy buzz. "Do you want me to turn it off?"

Max didn't answer.

Rich snapped on the lamp at the end of the couch and moved to switch off the television. Max seemed to blink. He looked down and around the apartment. It looked different in the light. He made an observation. "You cleaned up."

"Yeah."

"You didn't have to."

Rich shrugged.

"So what did you find?"

Rich looked at him.

A faint, very faint smile creased Max's lips. "Nothing?"

Rich got up. He had been sleeping in a pair of jeans and a mostly unbuttoned shirt. "Can I get a soda?"

"Why not?"

Rich walked into the kitchen, got a can of cola from the refrigerator, and walked back out. Max was still sitting in his chair, facing the couch. "I said you could stay here, Rich. I didn't give you a warrant to search."

Rich held his soda tight in his fist. He frowned. "I didn't search."

"I think maybe you did. After."

"After you left?"

"I meant after you found the bag."

Rich slumped back on the couch. Max produced what he had been concealing under his leg. The small black shaving kit.

Rich had seen it before.

Max grimaced. "I guess I was in too much of a hurry. I guess I left it in the bathroom."

"On the sink," said Rich.

Max nodded, ever so slowly, his eyes dull.

Rich popped the tab on his cola and tried to be sarcastic, although he felt just a little afraid. Of what? He asked, "How did you ever get by without them?"

"You'd be surprised."

"Aren't you going to tell me everybody smokes grass? Aren't you going to tell me it's no big deal?"

"I wish I could."

Rich thought about it. "You surprised me. I thought you were different."

"I am different."

"You're just like everybody else. After kicks."

"You think I'm a junkie?"

Rich shook his head. "I don't think anymore."

"Why is that? Have I ever offered you drugs? Have you ever seen me offer anyone drugs?"

"Maybe you don't like to share."

Max laughed. It sounded forced.

Rich shook his head. "Take a look at yourself."

"Why?"

"What happened to you? You left here in those same clothes. You haven't shaved."

"Consider me on vacation."

"Right." Rich collapsed on the couch again and took a sip of the soda. A small one. "This whole place if full of drugs," he told Max then.

"I have allergies."

"They didn't look like allergy pills to me."

"How could you tell?"

Rich frowned. Good question. Or good diversion, maybe. "All the labels on the bottles are in Spanish. Where do you get your allergy pills from? Tijuana?"

"Monterrey, actually. I just rent a car in Laredo and drive right across the border. Look, they're my pills. Okay?"

Rich didn't have a chance to reply. Max got up and walked over to the small dining room, where a plant hung in the window.

Rich let his concern show through. He looked over and asked, "Do you really take those things? All of them?"

Now it was Max's turn to smirk. "I like a little variety. It's the spice of life, right? If one doesn't do the trick, maybe another will. Right?"

Rich watched as Max began to pace. Slowly, almost

134

not moving. He took an interest in the plant and at the same time asked, "Did you tell Jenny?"

"No."

Max looked relieved.

Rich sighed. "Are you killing yourself with those things?"

Max looked stricken. "God, I hope not." He turned back to Rich. "Go to sleep."

Rich tried. He lay back and listened as Max walked down the hall and locked himself into his bedroom. Rich lay under the light awhile, then switched it off. He wondered why he hadn't left the apartment Friday night, after he'd found the joints. After he'd found all the pills. He could have gone home, or found somewhere else to stay. But after thinking it over, he had decided not to leave a friend who was in trouble.

Finally, he managed to doze off. The sleep was not without dreams. Usually Rich suffered troubled dreams, but he was finding that the more disrupted his life became, the simpler his dreams were. Complex night visions had resolved themselves into events he could deal with. No longer was he pursued by sinister figures or plunging from sheer cliffs.

Tonight he dreamt of Jenny.

She was standing near him, in the parking lot of the Mall, shaking her head. "You'll never have a chance with me." Why? Had he really told her about finding Max's bag? He hadn't meant to. He might be jealous of her feelings towards Max, but it wouldn't be right to take advantage of Max's kindness by running to her with what he had found in the apartment. That would be just as wrong as fighting. Wouldn't it? So what had happened? It wasn't fair that he'd never have a chance with Jenny. It was a mistake to tell her, it was a mistake—

Rich awoke, embarrassed. Max was standing over him. It was still dark in the living room, but the hall bathroom light was on. Max had cleaned himself up and shaved. He wore a blue pullover. "Don't judge me until you know why," he said.

135

Rich pulled himself up, confused by the sudden awakening. Jenny had seemed so close, and now . . .

Max backed away and switched on the dining room light. Rich could see the clock now. It was barely six. No wonder he felt groggy. "What's wrong?" he asked.

"There are reasons for almost everything in this world. Even for what I do. For what I have to do."

Rich took a breath and held it. His teeth were gummy; they felt as if they were wearing little sweaters. He released the breath and said, "What are the reasons?"

"I don't have ready little answers to pass along," Max responded. "There is no quick explanation for why I need things. Get up and get ready. We're going for a ride."

Rich frowned. "You have a car?"

"It belongs to Karen."

Rich watched Max for a minute. He looked fine, but that was the problem. He looked too different from the zombie who had returned home just hours before. Rich asked, "Are you all right?"

Max frowned. "If you mean am I high, the answer is no. If you just wanted to know if I was all together, yes. I'm fine. Hurry up and get ready."

Rich stood up. "I have school today," he protested.

Max shook his head. "We all make sacrifices."

Rich took a fast shower and changed clothes, which was not easy since Gus had packed the suitcase for him in haste and with an almost total disregard for the necessities. Rich had plenty of socks and underwear, as the drawer had been emptied into the suitcase, but only three pairs of pants and two shirts. He selected a pair of clean jeans and a red checkered shirt. It made him look like a lumberjack. He followed Max out to the silver Chevy Chevette just as the sun was breaking, glowing weakly through the clouds, and it was nearing seven-thirty.

Max drove the car.

Although he had problems at first with shifting, Max adjusted very quickly. He found the back roads immediately and left Greylake as if he had no intention of ever going back.

Rich watched Max work the gears in between glances out the window. "This car belongs to Karen?"

"Yeah."

"Where is she?"

"Where she belongs. Away from this."

Max took Rich to a Launch Facility.

They came across it amidst a field of harvested alfalfa. A recently cleared dirt road snaked around the site, which was a concrete slab encircled by a twelve-foot-high chain link fence topped with barbed wire. The sign read, RE-STRICTED AREA. PROPERTY OF THE UNITED STATES AIR FORCE.

Max stopped the car on the dirt road and got out. Rich followed. Max walked up a bluff that overlooked the site, traipsing through the thin layer of snow that blanketed the grasses there. He pointed out the site as Rich joined him. "That is a missile."

Rich stood beside him and frowned. "I've seen one before."

"You mean that display on base?" Max shook his head. "Forget that. That one is a toy. A model of the real thing." Max pointed again. "What you can't see beneath that cement is the real thing. Three hydrogen bombs primed to go, atop the same kind of technology that put man on the moon. Climb the fence around the site, and you'll set off a dozen invisible alarms. The place would be swarming with Air Force cops."

Rich looked down at the site. The ultimate power in the world, and it looked like an enclosed parking lot. He glanced at Max. "Are we going to do it?"

"Do what?"

"Climb the fence."

Max looked up and down the horizon. The sky was gray, threatening more snow. High above, a hawk wandered by in search of his morning meal. Max shook his head and started back down to the car. "Not today."

When they got back in the car and buckled up, Max waited to start the engine. "You know that you're welcome to stay with me as long as you want," he said. "I just want you to know that running rarely helps."

"I was thrown out," Rich reminded him.

"Your dad has probably calmed down by now."

"So I should go back?"

Max stiffened his lip. "Never crawl. Talk."

"And say what?"

Max started the car. "Confront him with whatever it is that you're feeling."

They started winding around the dirt road again.

Rich looked out the window at the snowy fields. "What I'm feeling is that I was tossed out of my house with one poorly packed suitcase."

Max nodded. "He doesn't understand you. You don't begin to understand him. You should be working to understand each other."

"Why?"

"Because if you walk away from this one, you'll regret it for the rest of your life. Don't let your family chase you away. Resist."

"What do you mean, resist?"

"I mean it's better to die fighting than to let anyone just roll over you. If you find something wrong in this life and just go along, you're a lemming. A little mouse that hurls itself into the sea every few years. Stand firm and resist."

Rich wondered a minute. "Doesn't that sort of make you the same as the people you're resisting?"

"Never think that." Max turned the car back onto the blacktop and headed north. "If you refuse to think it, then it will not be so."

Rich looked away.

Max said, "You need to learn to appreciate yourself first. Forget about me, forget about anyone else. You need to like yourself first. That makes it really hard for others not to like you too."

"Is that what you do?"

Max looked at him, almost smiling. "Well, you know, I'm different. I'm a hard case."

They drove. Every few miles for the first day Max would find the right side road or gravel track and lead them to another missile, parked out in some field. They

138

all had blue metal identification signs posted on their gates. D-3. G-7. M-9.

Rich didn't see the point of the excursion, and he said so. They all looked the same.

"You're right," said Max. "You don't see the point."

They drove beyond five o'clock, looking at missiles. Once they drove past a site that was actually occupied by Air Force personnel: N-11. Three dark blue vehicles were parked on the launcher lid. Several heads turned as Max and Rich cruised slowly by. A lot of miles were put on the car that day, and they stopped twice for gas. Max picked up dinner at a burger place in Castle Rock and drove out so they could eat it on the access road of 0-8. Rich thought better than to question.

Instead of heading home as Rich expected, they drove farther north. Max didn't talk much, and he stopped unexpectedly at a gas station in Hardin. The tank was still over three-quarters full, and Max didn't pull up to the pumps. He hid the car beside the building and kept a tight grip on the steering wheel.

Rich looked at Max. The color seemed to be draining from his face even as he watched. It was frightening to see. "Are you all right?"

"I'm just tired. I need to stop in the bathroom."

"Wait a minute . . ." Rich had just noticed something. A bluish mark on the back of Max's left hand. A large bruise. Had that been there before? "What happened to your hand?"

"What?" Max examined it. "I think I banged it on the back of the car door."

"When?"

"It's not important. I'll be back in a minute." Max pushed himself out of the driver's seat. It seemed like an effort.

Rich watched him disappear around the corner of the station. What was going on? He tried to think. What was in those medical texts that he read on occasion? What did marijuana and pills do to you? Could they make you sick? Obviously. Could they make you bruise easily? Maybe.

139

Was he killing himself with those things?

Quite possibly.

Rich couldn't help but shiver. What was he supposed to do? Anything? Nothing? Should he tell somebody?

No. That thought was cold and immediate. He would not bring anyone else into it. Whatever happened about the drugs, whatever happened on this trip, it was between him and Max. And the only thing that could be done right now was to worry. A lot.

Rich waited. He switched on the interior dome light and started rifling through the glove compartment, looking for something to read while Max was inside. Karen's junk, mostly. The owner's manual for the car, the registration, a receipt for a new front tire. And one of Max's empty orange pill bottles.

Rich froze. That explained it. At dinner, when Rich hadn't been watching, Max had obviously swallowed whatever was in the bottle. And now he was reacting to it. So what was in the bottle?

Rich tried to read the label, without success. Like the rest, it was typed in Spanish. Wait. Almost all of it was in Spanish. Some looked like Latin, which made sense. Rich knew medical terminology was universal. Drugs and diseases all had Latin names so that no matter where your doctor was from, he could still talk about it with a doctor from America, or Russia, or Mars. What was the Latin name for the drug on the bottle? It was hard to tell: *daunomycin . . . vincristine . . . methyl GAG . . .*

GAG? What the heck was that?

Daunomycin? That sounded familiar. Rich snapped the glove compartment closed, keeping the bottle in his hand. Okay, Dr. McFadden. Work it out. What was familiar about the word? Then it occured to him. The previous summer, he had spent one fun-filled week suffering from strep throat. The doctor on base had prescribed an antibiotic to clear it up, and Rich had been interested to know that the antibiotic was called *streptomycin*. Weird name. The doctor had told him that there were a lot of different *mycin's*, depending upon what you had. They were all antibiotics.

140

Daunomycin. How the heck did you get high on an antibiotic?

Unless . . .

No drugs and alcohol. That was a big one, preached on television all the time. What about antibiotics and marijuana? What kind of a high did that produce? Yeah. And Max was still inside the men's room . . .

Suddenly Rich got very angry. He felt used. He stormed out of the car and ran over to the men's room. The door wasn't locked. He went inside. "Hey!"

There was no sign of anybody inside, but there were three enclosed toilet stalls. "Max!" The hollow-sounding men's room made Rich's voice seem harsh. Good. That was how he felt. "Max!"

A toilet flushed. "Yeah . . . Hold on . . ."

It was Max. He came out of the toilet stall, holding a crumpled paper towel near his mouth. "Get bored in the car? Problem?"

Rich held up the bottle. "I want to know what this is."

"An empty pill bottle. And?"

"And what is . . . daunomycin?"

"Crudely pronounced. It's an antibiotic."

"Oh." Rich had expected Max to lie about it. "What's it for?"

"It's for the flu. I get the flu a lot."

"And this cures it?" Rich was baffled; he had never taken anything stronger than aspirin for the flu.

Max shrugged and mumbled something Rich couldn't make out. "It makes your head spin," he added. "Sometimes your gums bleed. And it keeps you sick to your stomach."

"And the joints in the bag?"

"They keep me from being sick to my stomach all the time."

"Is that what's wrong now?"

"Well . . ." Max tossed away the paper towel and smiled. Or tried to. "I figured I wouldn't make a bad impression by getting stoned on this trip. So you'll have to excuse me if I throw up now and again."

141

"Are you going to be all right?"

"Absolutely. Just as soon as I get a little rest."

Rich nodded. "We should head back to Greylake."

"No. We're going to Missoula. I just need to catch a few hours sleep in the back seat."

In the darkness Rich sat awake in the front seat, trying to sort everything out in his head, while Max crashed behind him. Max slept for almost two hours, then awoke with a moan. He crawled outside the car, and Rich heard him retching. He disappeared into the men's room, then returned ready to drive. He looked terrible.

They drove farther north. Past Lewistown, Great Falls, and Shelby. Rich couldn't keep himself awake, and he found himself drifting in and out of sleep. It was hard to tell where reality ended and the dreams began. On occasion the car would jolt to a halt, and he would awaken staring at another missile site.

C-6.

J-4.

A-10.

Max drove on, almost crazed at times. Almost asleep at others. As Rich found sleep, one image occupied his dreams: a barbed wire pen containing steel and concrete and death.

He awoke with a start.

He felt as though he had been sleeping for days. Dawn was approaching on the horizon, and they were parked in front of another one. Max had the Chevette's lights reflecting off the RESTRICTED AREA signs of another gate. This one was called T-11.

"Tango Eleven," said Max.

Rich looked, slowly nodded, and suddenly he realized.

They were everywhere.

There was nowhere to run. There was absolutely no place in Montana to go where you would not be near a nuclear missile launch facility.

E-2.

F-7.

K-8.

"There are over a thousand of them across this part

of America," Max said. "Montana. Wyoming. Missouri. North and South Dakota."

"Like this? Everywhere?"

"Everywhere."

A few hours later, they arrived in Missoula.

Missoula, Montana was the home of the University of Montana. Rich had never been there. Max drove onto the campus and parked in front of a coffee house. He looked a hundred years older. He scratched at the stubble on his chin and said, "Come on inside."

Rich did, finding a seat at a back booth while Max paused at a telephone hanging in the corner. When he sat down, a waitress came over with a small green pad and took their lunch order. Rich got a bowl of chili, and Max ordered a small glass of soda. They were still waiting for their food when a bearded man entered the diner and looked the place over. He wore cowboy boots, jeans, a red shirt and a sleeveless sheepskin vest. His head was hidden by a large cowboy hat, but the waitress scolded him, and he removed it. He nodded to where Rich and Max sat and walked over.

Max stood and shook his hand. He gestured to Rich. "This is Rich McFadden."

Rich didn't know what exactly to do, but he stood, and the man took his hand in a firm grip. Rich saw that he was being appraised with a glance.

Max leaned against the table. "Rich, this beast here is Milo Tomikas. Majoring in . . . what? English?"

"Troublemaking," said Milo, the beast. He squeezed into the booth beside Rich and asked, "Spending much time in jail lately?"

"Not since January."

"But we're on for Christmas?"

"Let's not talk here," said Max. He explained that the Greylake STN office was under Air Force OSI surveillance.

Milo whistled. "Talk about your own private Watergate. If you could prove that, you could really roll some heads."

"Yeah, but who could ever prove it?"

"Something to consider."

143

"Why do you think I'm here?"

Milo nodded. "Okay." He pulled a pen and a small card from the shirt pocket beneath his vest. After scribbling a message on the back of the card, he slid it across to Max. Max lifted the card. "What's this?"

"Waylon's new address. He moved."

"What about everybody else?"

Milo shook his head a little, smiling. "What's it been, Max? A year?"

"A little more."

"You know how these things go. People go on with their lives."

"Except for some."

"Most of us don't count. We're still trying to graduate."

Max nodded. "Okay. Fill me in."

Milo shrugged. The food arrived, and Milo ordered a cup of coffee. Max sipped his soda, and Rich nibbled at the chili. It wasn't very spicy, more like bland beans and hamburger. Milo continued, "Well, you know about Stacey."

"I heard she was expelled."

"Yeah. She stayed in town for a while, working at K-Mart. Finally she went back west."

Max nodded. "Back to Los Angeles."

"Well, Max. How long did you expect her to wait?"

"I didn't expect her to wait."

Suddenly Milo rose. "I guess I'll see you at the house. Or will I?"

"What about your coffee?"

"Drink it for me. I've got to get to class." He sort of smirked. "This semester is my last chance to graduate."

Max nodded. "Okay."

Milo looked at Rich and extended his hand again. Apparently, he had come to a decision. "McFadden?" he asked.

Rich was startled. "Yeah?"

"I think you're all right. If you need help from the north, you come to me. Milo Tomikas. I'm pretty easy to find." He turned, pulled his hat on, and left. Max watched him go, then left a five dollar bill on the table and said to Rich, "Let's go."

They killed a good part of the afternoon, going several places and seeing some people but rarely staying anywhere more than ten or fifteen minutes. At one stop Max parked the Chevette near a red brick house with the number 15 on its door. It was a pretty rundown neighborhood; the house next door had a Ford up on blocks amid the uncut grass of the front lawn. Three kids raced by on bikes, popping wheelies on the sidewalk. Max rapped twice on the door.

A big-faced man with a Fu Manchu mustache answered. He was about Max's age. "I don't believe it," he said, shaking his head.

"Believe what?" said Max.

"Get yourself in here!"

Max waited until they were in the sparsely furnished living room before introducing Rich to the man, who was named Waylon Kirby.

Waylon turned to Rich and said, "Hope and peace with you, Rich. And if not, then survival."

Rich didn't say anything. He was too busy watching the girl on the couch.

She was Rich's age, at best eighteen if you chose to stretch the point. She had shimmering blonde hair which had been braided and released, causing it to puff and frizz. She was wearing jeans and a maroon sweater and no shoes. Waylon Kirby gestured in her direction. "Debbie, say hello to Max and Rich. They're here to carry the war to society."

Max half nodded and looked at Waylon. "I have a security problem developing."

"With STN?"

"The Air Force has a plant working with us. Closely, I think. I'm looking for suggestions."

"Does it have to do with the December plan?"

"I think it might. Otherwise it's a hell of a coincidence."

Waylon nodded. "That it is."

"We should talk."

"Okay." Waylon looked at the girl on the couch. "Debbie? Could you monitor Rich's life enhancement for a few minutes?"

"Sure."

Max and Waylon traipsed upstairs. Uninvited, Rich stood waiting in the living room. "Do you like grapes?" Debbie asked him.

Rich stared at her.

"You look like someone who appreciates a good grape."

"Does grape Kool-aid count?" Rich asked stiffly.

"Kool-aid? You mean like with sugar?"

"Sort of."

Debbie thought a minute. "Do you know Milo Tomikas?"

"Yeah."

"I thought so."

"Why?"

"You guys seem just like Milo. You're up to something, aren't you?"

How the heck should I know, Rich wondered. He shifted on his feet. "Maybe."

Debbie smiled at him. "You are."

"Are you Waylon's sister?" he asked, changing the subject.

Debbie giggled.

Rich frowned. "What's the deal?"

"I'm his live-in."

"Live-in? You mean his girlfriend?"

"I like to think so. Mostly I feel like maid and bottle-washer."

"How old are you?"

Again, Debbie smiled. "No comment. How old are you?"

Rich felt instantly sick. Not because of the situation between Debbie and Waylon—or what it seemed to be—but because of what it implied about Jenny's obsession with Max. And Max's obsession with Jenny.

Did she want to be his "live-in?"

Debbie gave Rich a wave, inviting him over to the couch. "Sit down, take a rest. They won't be done for a while."

146

Stomach still churning, Rich sat down on the opposite end of the couch. Debbie moved quickly, though, and Rich was overwhelmed by exciting smells: perfume, grapes, and the very human smell of someone close. She whispered deviously, "I know what you guys are doing."

Rich tried to smile back. He was afraid Max and Waylon would reappear and find her hanging on him. At the same time, it was the single most exciting feeling he had ever had in his entire life. He wanted her to back off, but he didn't want her to leave. He tried to sound confident. "What are we guys doing?"

"You're going to take over a missile."

Rich almost shrugged. Occupy a site, not exactly news. He had anticipated as much. Still, he felt very important just then. Obviously Debbie thought he was one of the brains of the organization, and she admired him for it. "What are you going to do when you get in?" she asked.

Rich did shrug this time. "No big deal."

"It will be. I want to be there when you break those locks."

"Locks?" Rich hadn't seen any big locks on the fence.

"Waylon found that ex-Air Force guy. The one who's helping you get past the alarms. Into the site. I want to be in the silo with you when you pull the missile apart."

Rich felt his blood temperature fall fifteen degrees. "Pull it apart?"

Debbie laughed, a shrill giggle. "Scratch one. Stop the Nightmare for Christmas. Right?"

Rich looked at her, stunned.

They were doing what?

Oh, my God.

What was he supposed to do now?

Max came back in the room. "Rich, it's time to start back."

Rich nodded. "Yeah."

They drove back to Greylake through a more direct route. Max drove without pause, stopping only for gas and sodas. Around four-thirty it grew dark. Max switched on the headlights and continued driving. It began to snow; small, dense flakes fell off and on throughout the night.

147

Rich dozed occasionally, and when he was awake, he watched the snowfields.

They were about ninety miles from Greylake, according to the last sign, when Max pulled the Chevette down a side road. Rich prepared himself for another moody pass by a missile site, but he spied something else in the glow of the headlights. A hill.

Max stopped and pulled up the parking brake. He pointed up the paved road which led to the top of the hill. "That's where they stay."

"What?"

Max gestured again, and Rich looked. This time there was no mere outline of a concrete launcher behind the fenceline; this time there was a mini-installation. The fence surrounded a dark green building and garage.

"What is it?"

Max shook his head. "Launch Control Facility November One." He looked devastated. "Ninety feet below that building, encased in a glass capsule, is the missile combat crew. The guys with the actual firing keys to all of those missiles. They could light up the world."

Rich looked at Max, who looked like nothing more than a representation of living death. "Are you all right?"

"No, I'm not all right. I'm dying. We're all dying. Of all the people in the world, nobody should know that we're all dying any more than the two guys down there with those firing keys. They know. But they still keep coming out here."

Rich looked at Max a long while in silence, and finally he nodded. "Is that why you take the pills and stuff?"

"I'd do anything to stop this pain of dying."

Eighteen

Jenny suffered the dream, tossing and turning, and finally tore herself awake.

She wasn't alone in her room.

She recognized the shadow in the doorway. "Wesley?"

"Jenny? You all right?"

Jenny breathed. Buttoned down. "Yeah. I'm okay."

"You yelled something."

Jenny swallowed in the dark. Had she cried out? What? "And you heard?"

"I was across the hall. In the bathroom."

"What time is it?" Jenny asked because the Hairy Werewolf was blocked by a stack of textbooks.

"It's late," said Wesley. "Everybody else is in bed."

Jenny said nothing.

"Are you tired?"

"Yes," said Jenny, although she doubted she would be sleeping soon. Her heart still pounded a rough beat. "Good night."

"Jenny? Christmas is coming. Don't be sad."

Jenny nodded in the dark. "I won't."

Wesley pulled the door shut, and Jenny closed her eyes. The tears came, hot and sticky, and Jenny muffled the sound with her pillow, but she couldn't stop them.

For the first time in a long time, almost as long as she could remember, Jenny cried herself to sleep.

The next morning she woke up early, but only the sun startled her. There were no upsetting sounds coming from downstairs, although everyone seemed to be awake already. Jenny slid from bed and examined herself in the bathroom mirror. The verdict was clear: she was a mess. She took a quick bath, washed her hair, and dressed herself. She put on pink trousers with a gathered waist and a matching pink and grey woven-check shirt. Looking smart, she thought. She snapped on the belt and went downstairs for breakfast. After she finished her cereal and milk, she went back upstairs to work on her poem.

It was the poem she had started already, before her life at Stop the Nightmare. It had no title yet. She remembered her thoughts of Max when she had first seen him speak at school and at the first STN meeting. She had ignored the message then and wondered about the messenger. She had questioned his motives. Now she knew the messenger almost as well as she knew the message. But did she understand the motives yet? Did she know the real reasons?

Jenny finished the poem:

> *He stood his ground until an army came*
> *and ground him where he stood.*
> *They took his horse, his money of course*
> *and hung him minus hood.*
> *His eyes were blue, his words were two*
> *he said them as I would.*
> *They jeered him for staying, for dying*
> *For praying*
> *Asking Who Could Save Him?*
> *And he replied*
> *as he died*
> *"You could."*

Jenny hesitated. Okay. What next?

Captain Daddy spoke from the doorway. He hadn't knocked, or at least she hadn't heard. He seemed angry. "Kirk just called. He said he found out where you've been spending your afternoons when you've been cutting school. He thought I should know."

Jenny chilled, then looked at her father. He stepped into the room. "Jenny?"

"Yeah."

"Is that all you have to say? Yeah?"

Jenny shrugged. Court, she figured, was no longer in session.

Captain Daddy sighed, sitting now on the corner of the bed. "Jenny, what is going on?"

"What?"

"You know what I mean. You suddenly skipping school. Why is that?"

Jenny sighed. "I didn't feel like going."

"I don't believe that."

"I found something. Okay?"

"What do you mean, you found something?"

"Somebody has to work for peace. Don't they?"

"I think it's a little outrageous to think that the cause of world peace can be helped by your skipping school."

Jenny looked away.

"Besides all of that, have you ever stopped to think about the kind of trouble you could get me into?"

"How would it affect you? It's not you doing it."

"The Air Force doesn't look at it that way."

Jenny closed the notebook she had been writing in. "It's nobody else's business."

"It's not that simple."

"Why? Why isn't it that simple?"

"I don't know," said Captain Daddy. He took a breath. "I don't know a lot of things anymore."

"Like what?" Jenny tried to look accusing.

"How did you get involved with this anti-nuclear stuff? Was it that guy at school who spoke to your class? I've been hearing about that ..."

Jenny thought of the motives of the messenger. She asked her father, "Have you ever really considered what it is that you do for a living?"

"I serve my country."

"How could you ever defend killing a hundred million people?"

Captain Daddy stared a long silent moment. When he finally did speak, his words were calm, but there was an edge to his voice that Jenny didn't understand. "I don't feel as if I need to have this particular conversation with my daughter."

151

Jenny nodded. "You've never really thought about it, have you?"

"Jenny, it's not something you think about. You don't think about it because you're always thinking about it. It's always there, staring you in the face from the lockbox with the keys in it." Captain Daddy shook his head. "My God, Jenny, do you think this is all part of some plan? Wait for the 'Go' signal and then nuke the world? We're out there trying to deter a nuclear war."

"By building more and more bombs?"

"Jenny, we all have kids and lives of our own. My God." His hands shook with his words now. "Do you think for a minute that the Soviets would leave us in peace if we weren't constantly prepared to deliver massive retaliation? Don't you know how our defense system works? I'll explain it. Any attack on us, and they all die. Period. Any attack by us on them, and we all die. That is the system, Jenny. That's the way it's been for over forty years. And I have yet to hear anyone come up with a real alternative, besides surrender."

"No alternative?" asked Jenny.

Captain Daddy shook his head. "None."

"But what if we all die?"

Captain Daddy froze in his position and then seemed to shake himself free. He nodded and did something he almost never did at home; he gave an order. "Don't go near that place again."

Jenny got up and started for the door.

"Where are you going?"

"Not *there*," said Jenny. "Don't worry. I won't get you into trouble today."

Jenny bounded down the stairs, but Captain Daddy called from the top, "I want to know where you're going."

Jenny looked back. "I told you yesterday. I'm going to the museum."

She almost went to Marcie's house. Almost. That was where she usually went to escape bad things at home. But that escape opened up a lot more than she wanted to deal with. She hadn't actually been to Marcie's house in weeks. The distancing that had started with Patty was extending

152

to Marcie. At first it hadn't bothered Jenny that much. Patty had always been questionable as a friend, hadn't she? The Wing Commander's daughter? How close could you get to a person like that? Now Patty hardly talked to Jenny anymore, except when Marcie was around. Marcie always had been the center, the true friend. Now even she seemed tired of asking Jenny to do things, only to be turned down. They didn't even talk on the phone anymore. The deeper Jenny sank into STN, the further she drifted from her friends. Was that supposed to happen?

Jenny went to the museum instead.

Greylake, Montana had only one museum. A Western institution dominated by frontier art, the K. L. Jordan Art Museum was named in honor of Kyle Lynn Jordan, a Montana artist who had painted Western scenes in the early nineteen hundreds. Jenny liked to lose herself among the corridors there. She didn't walk the halls for the sculpture or mosaics of Western style "modern art," but she could contemplate a single painting for hours. She searched out details on the canvas, imagining poems about them. Jenny had imagined a lot of poems there since first finding the museum, but of all the paintings in the museum, none affected her like the lonely image of "Without Fail."

Jenny paid her dollar donation at the door and stepped into the cavernous entrance hall. There, waiting for her by a life-sized sculpture of a falling horse and rider, was Max. He was wearing the same rumpled sweater and jeans that he had worn in the sociology classroom. His eyes looked dark and tired now, but there was a mischievous twinkle in them all the same. Jenny slowed the pace of her walk, but Max stepped forward and met her halfway.

"I called your house," Max said in answer to the obvious unspoken question. "Your mother said you would be down here."

"My stepmother," Jenny corrected.

Max seemed taken aback. "Sorry. I think she thought I was someone else."

Probably Kirk, thought Jenny. Sometimes Max did affect just a trace of the all-American boy in his voice. "When did you get back?" she asked.

"A few days ago."

"How was home?"

"Adequate. How was your Thanksgiving?"

"Adequate."

Max smiled. "Just?"

"Barely."

Max looked around the entrance hall. "I've never been here before. They charged me a buck at the door, so I better see something worth a dollar before I leave. Want to show me around?"

Jenny stepped back. She felt unnerved by the *suddenness* of almost everything Max did. Sudden exits. Sudden appearances. What was next? A sudden trip to Brazil followed by a sudden appearance in the seat next to her in algebra class?

She led him around the museum. "I only look at the paintings," she said.

Max was examining a small metal carving of a group of men and their animals surrounding a campfire. "Any reason you don't like the sculpture?"

Never having had to explain her natural preference before, Jenny took a moment to think. Then she said, "The stone is too cold, and the metal workings seem manufactured."

"Manufactured?"

"Like they were bolted together from molds in Taiwan to sell to the tourists."

Max smiled and looked around again. "Is there anything in here that doesn't have a horse in it?"

"Yeah. I'll show you."

Jenny led him down another hall towards the stairs. "I should have brought Rich down to see this," Max said. "I asked him to come with me, but he seemed bothered by it."

"Why?"

Max shrugged. "I don't know. He said he didn't want to trouble you."

Jenny started down the stairs. So Rich was annoyed with her. Certainly he hadn't skipped three days of school

154

over that. Did he ever intend to come back? "How is he?" she asked.

"He's fine. He's out at the apartment. Why don't you stop by and see him sometime?"

"I'll see him in school."

"He's a good guy."

"Yeah," agreed Jenny. "He is a good guy."

Max paused in front of an especially gaudy painting. He grimaced and asked, "What was the artist thinking when he painted this?"

"Mostly about finishing it before lunch," Jenny answered.

Max laughed.

"My dad knows about me and STN."

Max looked at her. "For how long?"

"He told me today."

"How did he find out? Was it OSI?"

"Better than that. Somebody from school called my house."

"You mean the school office? Because you were skipping?"

"No. It was just somebody who wanted to be my friend."

Saying nothing, Max turned his eyes back to the ugly picture. "You still owe me about eighty-five cents worth," he murmured after a moment.

That shocked Jenny. She had expected him to question her more: Had she, too, been kicked out of her house? Would she have to quit STN? She sighed and took him to see "Without Fail."

They stood together at the end of the narrow hall in front of the painting. Max was staring harshly at it, and she feared he would criticize it or make some joke, but he didn't. Jenny herself became lost in the image again. The painting showed a man who had reached the summit of some great peak. He stood bloody and bruised, eyes looking not forward over the fantastic view of creation he had earned for himself but rather back to his climbing partner who struggled yards behind him. It was the detail of the man's face which most absorbed Jenny. She could

155

almost read what he was thinking, and she was troubled by what those thoughts appeared to be. *Go back*, his face screamed. *It's a disappointment.*

So many things were.

Finally Max spoke. He slowly nodded to the painting. "Yeah, that just about makes it." He seemed to sigh. "I always wanted to be the great adventurer. One of those wild men who do whatever they want and forget the consequences."

"You always seem to do what you want," said Jenny.

"Yes. But I never forget the consequences."

Max looked away, towards another painting that hung nearby in the small hall. It was a poor comparison to "Without Fail," but it had nice colors. Jenny had spent some time with it before, as a diversion. Max acknowledged the painting by saying, "There is a demonstration planned against the base. A big one."

"Is that why you looked for me?"

Max turned back to her and shook his head. "No. Not really. I just wondered how you felt about it."

Jenny hesitated. "It's important."

"Yes. But how do you feel about it?"

"I don't know. I really don't." She looked away from him, but there were really no more interesting pictures to contemplate. "You want to be the great adventurer. I'm not sure what I want to be. Or even what it is I'm supposed to be."

"Okay." Max stepped up alongside her. "In that case, where is it you want to be?"

"Where?"

"Yes. A location."

"I want to be with you."

Having something *sudden* happen right back at him seemed to unbalance Max just a bit. He looked closely at Jenny. She felt her insides tighten, but she wasn't sorry for having said it. For having felt it.

Max didn't say anything at all for a long moment, and then he said, "Eventually I'll be leaving this place. For a long time. I may not be back."

"Take me with you." It was an impulsive statement,

156

but again she made it. Jenny was tired of being so controlled. So buttoned down.

Max shook his head. "Jenny, I would be lying if I said I didn't feel some of those things for you. Special things. But some of the places I'm going to are . . ." He let his voice trail off.

"I want to go with you."

"Jenny, you can't."

"Why?"

"Because you have a lot more here to leave than you realize. It may seem like something easy to walk away from, but it's always harder to come back. Believe me. It may take years, but eventually you'll want to come back."

Jenny watched him. She wanted to blurt out something that would make him talk, that would make him explain what special things he felt for her. Max's voice interrupted her thoughts.

"Some of the places I'm going to, I can't even say for sure what it takes to get there."

He started to leave the small hallway. He had just reached the end when Jenny stopped him by saying, "I had a dream last night."

Max turned to face her. "Everybody dreams, Jenny."

"I had a dream that we were in a forest. You and I. And the wood was on fire. We wanted to get out, to escape from it, but we couldn't tell directions. Nobody around us knew where the fire began or ended."

Max said nothing.

"I have a lot of dreams."

"All bad?"

"Lately I'm always lost in them."

Max shook his head. "It's not love, Jenny."

Jenny looked hard at him. Her eyes were wide, and her throat felt tight. "It must be."

Max shook his head again. "It's not. Even if I wanted it to be, it's not."

Jenny sniffed and held it back. She stood there.

"Jenny, my entire life has been the end trying to justify

its means." He walked back over to her. "You know something about me that nobody else in the world does."

Jenny sniffed again. She felt crazy inside. "What?"

"I am nothing."

Jenny shook her head, feeling angry now. "You are the only person I ever met in my entire life who *was* something."

"Jenny, my life has been a game. I'm the little kid who doesn't have to grow up. It's easier that way. Puppy love, loose commitments. Did you know that it's easier for me to scream about the nuclear arms race in front of a thousand people than it is for me to call my father and tell him that I love him?"

Jenny felt the need to touch Max somehow, but she was also sure that if she did he would move away. She waited.

Max shook his head and slid back against the wall between two paintings. He rested his head back and looked so very tired now. He held a breath and then gave it up. "Sometimes I wonder if I'm even real."

Nineteen

Rich reflected on life within a house of cards.

On the surface, he was maintaining it. He was still staying at Max's apartment, but he was back at school. His brother Mike had brought him some things from home, so he was a bit more comfortable. He had a lot of time to catch up on his homework.

Max didn't seem to care that Rich knew he was smoking marijuana, but for some reason he worried that Rich would misunderstand the reason for the pills. "I'm prone to infections," he said. "Ever since I was a kid. No big deal." Still, he seemed especially petrified that Jenny would find out.

"You know her type," Max said one night on the way to the STN office. "I don't want her feeling sorry for me, or bringing over a pot of chicken soup."

Chicken soup. Right. Rich didn't think it was likely, not since Jenny had lost all interest in Stop the Nightmare and everyone in it, but he tried not to ruffle the walls of the house of cards. A misplaced remark might topple everything that took so long to build.

Living with Max was proving to be much quieter than Rich had anticipated, but it also put him in the position of watching the rapid changes Max went through. He seemed to begin each day near collapse, struggling to stay awake and growling out one-word sentences. Then would come his trip to the bathroom, supposedly to clean up for the day. Minutes would pass, and a new Max would appear—bright, cheerful, ready for action.

159

The weird shifts from sullenness to excited action scared Rich, but he didn't like to dwell on the cause of these mood swings. He couldn't believe it was the pills. Most of them seemed to be antibiotics, which Max said were for his infections. One exception was a bottle Rich found with the word *hematoglobulin* on the label. Rich knew that *hemoglobin* was blood, and the words seemed almost the same. Max said they were iron pills. "I take them instead of eating liver." He admitted he was anemic, but said it was because of all the junk food he ate.

Rich did worry about it. Something was obviously wrong. There was, of course, the stash of marijuana to consider. Was this what that stuff did to you? How could a cheap high be worth all the terrible side effects? Was Max addicted? Was the combination of pills and grass killing him? Rich wanted to call someone and ask. He went so far as to dial the local Helpline, but hung up the phone when a woman answered. It was a pathetic situation, but try as he might, Rich could think of no way to help that didn't seem like a betrayal. Here he was, working each night after school to save the world, and he couldn't lift a finger to save Max.

Life pressed on.

Rich realized the old line was true: The more things changed, the more they remained the same. He was on his own now, away from home, but at school he was still flip-out Rich. He didn't even have Jenny to talk to anymore, which was not to say that he had anything to say to her. She tried speaking to him in the hall once, but he felt weird listening to her and just squeezed past. As bad as it seemed, he couldn't help but wonder if she was part of Max's problem. Maybe her leaving was just one more of a long list of betrayals. If Rich tried to stay close to her, wouldn't that be a betrayal of Max as well?

Rich preferred not to think about Jenny. After finishing his homework, he concentrated on something else Mike had managed to smuggle out for him, his journal, the *Lonerman's Notebook*. He was months behind on the entries. He started to correct the situation by trying to tell what was happening to him, but that was quickly turning the book into a volume of regrets.

No.

But what else could he write? What else was true?

Rich thought hard. His first impulse, as always, was to dismiss major pain as irritation. Write down, "What a bummer," instead of really being honest. That was one of his regrets. He regretted not telling the truth about so many things. He regretted not being able to find some way to help Max. With life as fragile as it was, hesitation and fear had no place in it. That realization struck home especially hard. More and more his regrets were centering around Jenny, and the dull hollow feeling that she had left with him.

The feeling was like slipping into a hole, and then becoming the hole.

Rich honed and sharpened one regret to the point where the mere thought made him crazy. Like many others, it concerned the night he and Jenny went to the movie together. There had been a moment there, crossing the great parking lot, when Rich might have tried to kiss her. More than likely she would have stepped back quickly to avoid allowing their lips to touch. Probably she would have shoved him back with a flip remark. Probably she would not have let him near her.

But what if she had? What if she had stepped to meet him halfway, their mouths coming together?

The thought made him crazy.

He found the nights were getting longer again, and it wasn't exactly the sort of thing he could talk to anyone about. Of all his desires in life, of all his tabled regrets, the one that pained him the most was the fact that he had not even tried to kiss Jenny Westphal.

He distracted himself with Stop the Nightmare.

November in Montana gave up its ghost, and it became December in Montana. Holiday bells and plastic holly were appearing on lamp posts and at almost every street corner in downtown Greylake. Garish silver trees and multicolored lights decorated the Mall, and a fat Santa Claus had his photograph taken with the kids while seasonal music blared from every loudspeaker. Even Travers Air Force Base was taking on its own touch of Christmas. In mid-December Stop the Nightmare decided to bring Travers another touch of Christmas, in the form of a demonstration.

The day of the demonstration, Saturday, December 21st, was colder by midafternoon than at the day's harsh beginning, but at least the earlier icy rain had stopped for a while. The pavements were stained dark from the wet weather, and the roads were growing slick, but this had not stopped over four hundred people from marching from the First Fellowship Church of Greylake to the main gate of Travers Air Force Base. The march was part of a general protest over the presence of nuclear weapons in Montana.

Dressed in his heaviest jacket, Rich marched with the crowd. His large STN ORGANIZER button set him apart as a person the others could come to with questions. Blue and white PEACE NOW! placards dominated the crowd, but some people had hand lettered their own variations: SAVE THE CHILDREN! and ABSOLUTELY NO NUKES! and WHAT ABOUT TOMMOROW? Rich slipped through the crowd, walking faster to catch up with the blue Ford pickup truck which carried the portable podium and public address system. The truck was plastered with signs and banners, the most prominent being STOP THE NIGHTMARE.

Max was walking alongside the pickup, conferring with the driver, who turned out to be Milo Tomikas from Missoula. A few familiar faces from Missoula had shown up that morning to help out, and Rich was surprised when Waylon remembered his name and seemed genuinely happy to see him. Comrades in the cause, Rich thought. Aside from the Missoula volunteers, Rich was surprised at how many families with children had shown up for the long walk. It was five miles to the base, at least. After a few minutes' consideration of the matter, Rich thought he saw the point of bringing the kids. Despite the difficulty involved, some of the message would have been lost had the families chosen to leave their children at home. As for himself, Rich was used to walking.

As Rich threaded through the crowd, Milo greeted him first, raising a hand from the steering wheel while he navigated the crawling truck. The pickup set the pace for the walk, moving so slowly that sometimes it seemed to be parked. Rich went up to the cab to say hello. Milo smiled. "McFadden, how you doing? You feeling up for this?"

"Yeah."

Milo nodded back at him, keeping one eye forward on the road. His cowboy hat was cocked at an odd angle, and he had an almost suspicious smile on his face. "I hear you."

What did I say, Rich wondered.

Max turned around now. "I guess I better go keep track of Reverend Lowell," he said. He started to pull away but stopped to squeeze closer to Rich. "Did Jenny ever show up?"

Rich looked at him. Max's eyes were heavy and dark. There was something else, a small bruise on the side of his head, barely noticeable, on his left temple above his eye. The bluish mark disappeared under his hair. Rich swallowed. "Are you all right?"

Max placed a hand on Rich's arm and asked again, "Did Jenny ever show up?"

Rich frowned and shook his head. "No. But Karen is up ahead somewhere. She's looking for you."

Max cleared his throat. "Yeah, I know." He moved away.

"Max looks really tired," Rich said to Milo.

Milo shook his head. "Let me tell you something. That man never gets tired."

"Everybody gets tired."

Milo looked at Rich a moment, then relented a bit. "Maybe."

Rich turned, looking for Max. Why all the continued interest in Jenny? Obviously, Max was worried about her, worried about what she might do. One thing was painfully obvious—Jenny was all he thought about.

Rich shook his head. Join the crowd.

About three miles into the march, the singing started.

Initially, there had been problems trying to keep everyone on the road from trampling into each other, but that worked itself out. When the singing first started, Rich hesitated to join in, but the mood was contagious. It was a sincere, if not sensational, chorus. They started with Christmas carols, since the mood was high, and as they neared the base, they slid into a variation of an old John Lennon song about giving peace a chance.

When they reached the base, they grouped in a lot across the road. Then something odd happened. The crowd's number seemed to swell. A hundred people appeared out of nowhere. They were separated from the base by a dividing access road, and from where they stood, they could watch either the Travers AFB Main Gate or another lot across to one side. It was there that a counter-demonstration was setting up. Rich knew that the nervous front rank of marchers were those who had decided to perform an act of "passive civil disobedience"; they would cross the white line onto the base and be immediately arrested.

For a moment Rich flirted with the idea of crossing the line himself. But he knew things would go badly for Dad if he did, and, despite what had happened, he had no desire to ruin his father's career with a wild act of rebellion.

Reverend Lowell climbed onto the back of the pickup and activated the microphone. "How are you all doing?" he asked.

The response was applause and some cheering, but there were also boos and some shouted remarks from the counter-demonstration. Although small by comparison to the STN crowd, they definitely intended to be heard.

Reverend Lowell ignored the hecklers and went on with his speech. "We've come a lot farther than a few miles to say these things today. We've come all of our lives to be here today."

The counter-demonstration grew more agitated as Reverend Lowell spoke. Max seemed tense. Rich followed him as he left his position beside the pickup and moved toward the edge of the crowd.

"Hey!" someone standing next to Max shouted at the counter-demonstrators. "Why don't you morons shut up?"

The hecklers called back, using a stream of profanities.

Max said nothing; he just glared across the road. For some reason this seemed to unnerve the hecklers. "Go back to Russia!" a few of them yelled.

Rich looked at Max again. His eyes were glass. Or ice. "What are you doing?"

"Memorizing faces."

Without warning, one of the counter-demonstrators broke from his group. Before anyone on either side could react, he slammed forward into Max. Rich heard the grunt as air rushed from Max's lungs and he was knocked back onto the ground. The attacker punched and pounded Max. There were a few scattered screams, and now, finally, Reverend Lowell broke off in mid-sentence. The attack was in full view of the line of Air Force cops, but their jurisdiction ended at the white line, and they made no move to interfere.

Max made no effort to defend himself.

Milo Tomikas dived in and pulled the attacker off, pushing and shoving him back but not taking any shots at him. The leaders of the counter-demonstration recovered their man and slapped him on the back in approval. Max was helped to his feet. His face was cut and bleeding. "I'm all right," he said, waving assistance away. He met Rich's eyes for only a moment before turning.

Rich thought: *He didn't fight back. Why?* Second thought: *Neither did you. Why didn't you help?*

The shame hit him like a wave.

Reverend Lowell stepped aside as Max climbed into the truck bed. He took the microphone and said, "These are the same people who declare that man will never use the bomb." He touched a finger to his lips; there was a trickle of blood. He smeared it, streaking his fingers red and holding them up to the crowd. "This is what they wanted. How much more? Where does it stop?" Max called to the counter-demonstrators. "How much more blood will it take to satisfy you?"

There was no reply; the crowd fell silent.

Max looked another moment, then seemed to lose faith. He climbed slowly down from the truck bed, stumbling a bit. Rich was there for him, but Max pushed him away. "Stay here. Help out Reverend Lowell. I've got to stop back by the apartment."

"Why? What's wrong?"

Max tasted the blood on his lips and raised his hand again. "I need to take care of this. It's not going to stop bleeding unless I take care of this."

"What?"

"I'll see you tonight. It's all right."

Rich watched him go. Suddenly, deep inside and all over, Rich was scared. How could he have been so stupid? Obviously there was something wrong with Max. Something serious.

At the Eighth Street STN office that night, Reverend Lowell wore a smile and balanced a drink in his hand. "I think we made our point," he said casually. "When the pictures appear, the story will be simple. A group of average Americans who said they have had enough. The madness stops here."

Rich heard him, but he wasn't listening. He was keeping his eyes open for Max, who had yet to appear. Rich had called the apartment earlier, with no success. He was ready to bum a ride across town with Milo Tomikas when Max appeared in the doorway, wavering. He seemed hesitant to step inside.

Rich squeezed his way through the people in the office and stood beside him. Max had a bandage affixed to the corner of his lower lip, and his eyes were hot, cutting around the room, but what struck Rich immediately was the fact that Max reeked. He wore that burnt rope smell of marijuana. He had obviously smoked a lot of grass before showing up. He was stoned out of his mind.

"Max . . ." Rich tried to talk to him.

Max didn't acknowledge him at first. Then he said, "Go stand by Milo."

166

"What?"

"I need you to go stand by Milo. We found out who the OSI plant is; I know who she is. You're not going to like it."

Rich swallowed. "She?"

Max closed his eyes, shaking his head as if to clear it. "Yeah. She."

Rich thought about it. It didn't make any sense, but he realized with acute horror that nothing about Max or STN ever really made much sense. He thought of Jenny and her problems with her father. Had she wanted to be some sort of hero with the Air Force? She had, after all, quit STN for no real reason. And what about her and Max? What was the truth about their relationship? Was she really the OSI plant, the informant? She had appeared on the scene at about the right time, but . . . What was the truth anymore?

"Go stand by Milo . . ." Max said again.

"Why?" Rich asked. "Am I going to be safe there?"

Max shook his head, slowly, without any thought. Then he cleared a path for himself to the front of the room. He rapped a fist on one of the desks for attention. "Excuse me!" he called.

A few people turned, but most were taking their time. Max was in no mood, though, and with a violent motion overturned the desk with a shocking explosion of noise. "I need one damn minute!"

That did it. The party stopped. Reverend Lowell turned, eyes wary. Rich swallowed. Attention focused up front.

"Originally, as some of you know, we had plans for next week to take a Christmas tree and gifts and set them up in the middle of a missile site. We had to drop those plans."

Rich shivered. Max was going to reveal Jenny. That was why he wanted her to show up. Obviously, Max had originally intended to reveal her in front of everybody, but now he would condemn her *in absentia*. Rich despised what Jenny had done, but this was something he didn't want to see. He started making his way back towards the door.

Max called out, "Why don't you tell everybody why we decided to cancel the site occupation, Karen?"

Karen? Was Max calling witnesses? What did Karen know about Jenny? A terrible thought occured to Rich, and he froze. Karen was still standing beside Reverend Lowell, but now she was half smiling, looking confused.

Max nodded. "You see, everybody, what Karen is forgetting now is that she warned the Air Force about what we were thinking of doing. She gave them everything. Names, dates."

Karen's smile faded.

Rich felt his mind reel. Karen? How could it be Karen? What about Jenny? Then he remembered his first night as an STN volunteer, Karen's many questions. Soon after that, he was kicked out of his house.

"Come on, Karen. Aren't you OSI?" Max taunted.

Karen still wore a half smile. Her lower lip may have quivered just a bit, but she said nothing. She twisted on her heels and started to leave, but Milo Tomikas was there. Milo blocked her path and quickly snatched away her purse.

"Hey!" she objected.

The others in the crowd seemed almost as upset by it all as Rich was. Max continued speaking to her. "What are you going to do now, Karen? Arrest me? We're civilians. You don't have any authority here."

Milo sifted quickly through her purse and pulled out a foldover wallet. He unfolded it for the crowd, revealing a badge. Milo read aloud: "Special Agent Karen Milhous, Air Force Office of Special Investigations."

No one spoke.

"Did your bosses tell you that what you were being sent to do was illegal?" asked Max, almost kindly. "Military Intelligence infiltrating a civilian group. Did they tell you that you might go to jail for that? I mean, this all sounds almost communist." Max laughed then, but it was a hollow laugh. "Did your bosses tell you how you got a seventeen-year-old boy tossed out of his own house? How do you feel about that?"

Karen said nothing in answer. She was trying to reclaim her wallet. Milo shoved back her purse but held the ID away from her. She seemed consumed with rage and frustration now, and she turned toward Max. "Why don't we tell all the family secrets, Neuger?" she shouted.

Max looked at her. Rich looked at Max. His eyes were blank. Rich took a breath.

Karen was sputtering words. "Why don't you tell these people how you flunked out of ROTC at Michigan State? Isn't that your real reason for hating the military?"

"Shut up." Max was casually dismissing her.

"Why don't you tell them what you keep in your little black bag at home?"

Max recovered from that quickly; his words were ice. "Shut up."

"What else can we talk about?" asked Karen. "How about the fact that you like to hang out with pretty little high school girls?"

Max jerked forward suddenly, seemingly unable to control himself. "I said shut up!" Milo Tomikas rushed to place himself between Max and Karen, but Max was moving already. For one terrible instant Rich realized that Max's eyes were killer's eyes. Max appeared ready to strike out at Karen, to lash at her, and he was yelling, "Shut up, shut your mouth you—"

Max froze, not moving, not speaking.

In that same instant he had noticed what Rich had also seen. Something that meant almost nothing to anyone else in the storefront. Jenny Westphal, standing in the open doorway.

Jenny's face was pale and tense, and she seemed to be barely holding herself together. She had apparently been watching for some time. Before either Max or Rich could react to her presence, Jenny shivered once and turned.

She was gone.

Twenty

Jenny rushed from the STN office.

Her mind screamed, but it wasn't the horror of the girl's words that stunned Jenny. It was Max. She had seen enough in his face to cause her to recoil, as if she had suddenly discovered a poisonous snake in her bed. This time the message in Max's eyes was all too clear.

Most, if not all, of what the girl had said was true.

Jenny stumbled down Eighth Street, nearly slipping on the wet pavement. Sleet had been falling intermittently for the last hour. She crossed the street and shoved her hands deep in her pockets. Her jacket, although heavy enough, was unbuttoned and hung open. She wasn't concerned about the cold.

She worried over time. She worried over losing track of time as her mind groped for a way to silence the buzzing in her head, but there was no way to track any loss. She hadn't even worn a watch. She stopped at the corner and shivered. She had never known the messenger; she had never understood the motives. Until now. The motives were bogus, and the messenger was a false prophet.

"Jenny, wait!"

Afraid of being followed, of being chased, Jenny spun towards the voice. Rich. Wonderful. Rich McFadden, still wearing that stupid STN button, charged at her, shouting, "Jenny! Hold up!"

Jenny shook a finger. "Stay away from me!"

"I need to talk to you!"

Jenny looked for someplace to run, but there was nowhere to go. She turned back and yelled, "No! Go away!"

Rich caught up with her under a streetlamp. "Jenny, I'm sorry . . ."

"Why? Are you somebody else too?"

"You know who I am."

"I don't know who anyone is anymore."

Icy rain had begun to fall, and drops were collecting on Rich's face. He wiped his eyes with his palm and said, "I'm sorry for not being able to understand you."

"Why?"

"I thought you hated us. Hated me. For a while I even thought you were an OSI spy . . ."

Jenny tried to laugh at that. "Oh. Wonderful. You thought I was a spy."

"Worse than that," said Rich. "I thought you might not like me."

Jenny looked into the black sky. The raindrops found her too, splattering her face and beginning to mat her hair. She looked at Rich and asked, "So who do you think I am now?"

Rich shrugged. "Just someone else I'll never get to know."

Jenny listened to him. She remembered him shoving by her at school. What was he thinking then? That she was an OSI informant? Or something else, something worse.

Was any of that important now?

Jenny bit her lower lip, trying to button down. She shook her head just a little. "Could you go away now?"

"No. We need to talk."

"About what?"

"About Max. There's something wrong . . ."

Jenny shook her head fiercely now. "Don't you know that you're not driving me crazy anymore?" Hot tears streamed down her face. She felt herself collapsing inside, slipping into a void that was becoming herself. *There was a razor in the bathtub.* Through her tears she shouted, "Don't you know I'm already crazy? I'm crying. Don't you know I'm not allowed to cry anymore?"

Rich looked pained. "Everybody cries, Jenny."

171

Jenny slammed out her arms, forcing him back. "Not me! Not me!"

Rich grabbed for her hands. They were slick with rain, and she pulled away from him. "I need to tell you about Max," he said.

"What about him?" Jenny screamed the words in a rush.

"I think he's sick."

"What?"

"Really sick. I think he's really sick."

Jenny took a breath, then another one. "Why do you think that?"

Rich closed his eyes, seeming to pause for thought. He wiped the rain from his face. Jenny reflected on all the agony she had caused so many people, up to and including Rich McFadden standing in the icy rain. Was she special, or did everyone sling pain and guilt around in his own way?

Rich said, "I see things . . ."

"Things?" Jenny blinked. Was it rain? Or tears?

"Around the apartment. Things."

"Like drugs."

"Special drugs, Jenny. You don't understand . . ."

"You don't need to defend me."

Jenny turned without thinking. Max crossed over to them. "I don't need anyone to defend me."

Rich shivered in the rain. "I wasn't defending you."

"So what were you saying?"

Rich seemed aghast. "What was I saying? Max . . ."

"Yes." He was with them under the light.

"You're still bleeding."

Max touched the bandage on his face. It was getting speckled with rain, but it was already dark with blood.

Rich shivered again. "That happened this afternoon. Why is it still bleeding?"

"It's like shaving. Some small cuts don't close up—"

"Don't lie."

Max looked surprised. Jenny held her breath, waiting. It seemed forever. Finally, Max said, "Okay."

"What's wrong with you?"

172

"I'm a little sick."

"A little?"

Max looked at Jenny. She felt his eyes. Why did Rich have to do this to him? Couldn't he see Max was in pain? "What happened to your face?" she asked.

"Just a fight," he said. "We got some more threats tonight, after the demonstration. There will probably be more—"

Rich cut him off. "How sick are you?"

Max sighed. "What is it that you want to hear?"

Rich swallowed. "I know some things. I'm not stupid."

"I never said you were."

"I know you bleed. You bruise a lot. You get sick to your stomach, and you take a lot of antibiotics. And you smoke grass."

Jenny looked at Max. Rich continued. "I think we're talking about some kind of cancer."

"Okay." That was all Max said.

"Is it bad?" Jenny cut in.

Max looked at Jenny. "Remember your dream?"

She felt her heart jump. "My dream?"

"About the fire in the woods. Where you and I were trapped?"

Jenny nodded. Nobody know where the fire began or ended. There was no way out.

Max said, "I knew where the fire was all the time. Does that tell you anything about me?"

Jenny shook her head in confusion.

"It'll occur to you. Eventually."

"What?" Jenny felt Max was ready to leave, and indeed, he had started to turn. "What will occur to me?"

He ignored the question. "Things are going to start happening for STN now. They probably won't need me to go to jail for a while; Karen the OSI agent will be in the papers enough. So you don't have to worry about Max the convicted felon. But even if you did, I'd rather have it that way. I'd rather have you hate me for something I'm not than pity me for whatever it is that I am."

"Why?" Jenny whispered, shocked and on the verge of tears again.

173

Max opened his arms. "Hey . . . Sometimes I'm lost; sometimes I'm found."

He turned and started walking back across the street, but he hesitated and said something to Rich. "Okay, Sherlock, here it is: Chronic granulocytic leukemia, but I'd appreciate it if you wouldn't do your term paper at school on it. As a matter of fact, I'd appreciate it if you wouldn't say anything at all about it."

Rich looked numb, as if he had been slapped. Jenny didn't understand. Leukemia? What was that about?

Max looked at them and shook his head. "It's a cancer of the blood cells. In the end it's incurable. No escape." He paused. "But you're both going to die of pneumonia if you don't get out of this freezing rain. Go on." He completed his turn and started across the street.

Jenny couldn't stand the pain on Rich's face, and she couldn't understand her own feelings. She started to call out to Max, to yell something to stop him, to make him stay and listen, but when she opened her mouth, somebody else's words came out.

"Hey, commie!"

Jenny didn't move. She felt a shudder go through her. The voice behind her sounded sick, twisted. She heard the footsteps on the wet pavement. Behind her, Rich watched them approach. Max stopped and turned.

Jenny forced herself around. Though incredibly nervesick, she knew the greatest danger would be keeping her back to the threat. A snub-nosed cowboy led two of his friends out of the shadows and into the yellow glow of the street lamp. "Remember us?" he asked.

Max stepped back beside Jenny and said, "Yeah, I memorized your faces."

The cowboy on the right nodded. "I left you a little something to remember me by."

"Yeah," Max said and touched the bandage on his face again. "And we got your phone call. Too bad you didn't have the guts to leave your names."

"Names?" said the center cowboy. "That's easy. I'm Steve; this is Zack on my left and Sherman on my right."

Max frowned, mocking. "Sherman, huh? Like the tank."

"Yeah. You got a problem with that?"

"I got a problem with guys like you in general."

Jenny knew a fight was coming, and the prospect terrified her. Was Max so upset that he wanted to become a martyr to the cause by being beaten up by three drug store cowboys? She looked at Rich, but his face was unreadable in the falling drizzle.

Steve was shaking his head. "I just don't understand. What kind of Americans are you people?"

"Same as you," said Max. "We still kick our dogs and watch *Gilligan's Island*."

Zack chuckled, and Jenny resisted again the impulse to run from that laugh. "You're a funny guy. I can't wait to hear you tell jokes without any teeth."

Sherman turned to Jenny and Rich. "You kids take off. You don't want to see this."

"Yeah," Max said. "Rich, take Jenny back up to the office and wait for me."

"No." As she seemed to do so often around Max, Jenny spoke on impulse.

"Go," Max ordered.

Jenny shook her head.

"Hey, sweetie," leered Sherman. "Are you just a commie tramp, or do you take on anyone?"

Rich exploded.

Jenny screamed instantly when she saw Rich move, and it had been a long time since Jenny had screamed. Rich crashed forward into Zack, and they both went down, slipping on the wet pavement. Not expecting the sudden attack, Zack took a moment under Rich's pounding fists before he struggled back.

"Rich, no!" Max was yelling. "Wait!"

Jenny hadn't seen the cowboys' weapons until now.

Rich was still on top of Zack, punching and slapping at his surprised face, when, with one fluid motion, Sherman produced a length of black steel and caught Rich square in the back.

This time the scream stuck in Jenny's throat.

175

She didn't recognize the steel. It might have been a small tire iron or a length of pipe. Regardless of what it was, the black steel snapped into Rich's back with a sickening thud, and Rich went stiff, as if he had been shot through with a thousand volts. Zack shoved him off with minimal effort and elbowed him harshly before standing up himself.

Max spoke again, very slowly. "Jenny, I want you to leave now."

Jenny shivered again. "No."

"It's okay," said Zack. "She can watch." He and Sherman stepped forward. Steve produced a knife from his jacket pocket and, with a flip of the wrist, exposed its long blade. The edge glistened.

Instinctively, Jenny took a step back.

She expected Max to follow, but he didn't. Max stepped forward to meet the cowboys.

Zack made his move, lunging.

Max made the way he sidestepped Zack look almost effortless. He brought his left hand down in a casual motion that made the viciousness of the blow he struck seem all the more shocking. He seemed almost to grip Zack by the neck before slamming him down into the concrete with a loud smack. Sherman went to swing with the steel, but Max somehow ducked it and brought his left foot up to catch Sherman against the face. The blow tossed him back and down. Screaming terribly, he dropped the steel and grabbed his jaw with both hands.

Steve, the cowboy with the knife, didn't seem worried. "I'm going to cut you up bad," he snarled.

Max shook his head. "I'm going to make you eat that knife, and maybe the iron too."

Steve moved.

Max seemed perfectly prepared to step forward and take the knife away, but for some reason he was being dragged to the ground. Jenny gasped when she saw why. Zack had not been knocked unconscious by his fall; he had merely been knocked down. Now he was tugging Max down by the left leg as Steve came on with the knife. Despite his continued moaning, even Sherman was starting to get up now. Max was trying to pull away from Zack, but it was a battle of strength against strength, and Max looked tired and sick in the rain.

Sherman was rising.

Steve was just about on him with the knife.

Jenny saw the black steel near her feet.

Sherman was almost up now, trying to come over.

Jenny reached and snapped the weapon up. It was heavy and solid.

Jenny knew why Sherman was moving to help Zack pull Max down. They were going to hold Max while Steve stuck him with the knife. Not thinking, she rushed up and slammed the heavy steel down across Sherman's back. He fell, his thick fingers seeming to fumble for something. He reached back for Jenny, but she brought the steel down hard again, and he stopped resisting.

Jenny heard Max grunt and turned in time to see him break free of Zack's grasp. He kicked out with his right foot, catching Zack square in the face. There was a wet, snapping sound as Zack flew back, but at the exact moment Max caught Zack in the face with his boot, Steve caught Max in the side with the knife.

The scream came now. Loud and shrill and terrible.

Only the source of the scream wasn't Jenny.

It was Max.

The blood was already gushing from his side as Max spun around. The knife slid deeper into him, but he smashed Steve in the face, throwing him back with a series of punches and kicks intended to keep him on the ground for a while.

Jenny dropped the steel. Groaning in an agony beyond that which could have been caused by the knife, Max attempted to straighten himself. He pulled the blade from his side; the blood flowed freely. Max seemed unconcerned now. He stepped over Zack and Steve to where Rich lay.

Jenny shuddered now. "Is he dead?" she whispered.

Max looked at Rich closely. "No." He took a breath. "His kind don't die easy."

Jenny looked down at Sherman. The tears were flowing

again, and she was beyond all buttoning down now. "I think I hurt this one real bad."

"Forget him."

"But I . . ."

Max grimaced and brought his left arm down to protect his side. "Go back to the office. Call the police and get an ambulance. I'll stay with Rich here until you get back . . ."

"You're bleeding bad. Rich said it doesn't stop—"

"Just go!" Max shuddered himself now, and the gesture terrified Jenny. She got up and ran. She looked back from across the street and saw Max whispering something to Rich's unconscious form. She hurried to the STN office and called the operator, who put her through to the police. Then an ambulance. Then she raced back outside.

Max was lying beside Rich, holding him. But Max was already gone. The first wailing of a siren could be heard in the distance.

Overhead, the drizzle had finally turned to snow. The flakes grew larger and began accumulating, even on the sidewalks and streets.

THE LAST PART

Twenty-one

Jenny watched from across the street as the Base Commander lit the lights of the official Travers Air Force Base Christmas tree. It was a twenty-five-foot pine trucked in from Canada. Nearby, bathed in white spotlights, stood a ninety-foot display model of a Minuteman III missile. The missile made the tree seem pointless. Jenny turned and walked away.

She managed to button down. She was not horribly upset, and she felt that was the key. Not being horribly upset. No matter what happened, she would not become horribly upset. She kept an eye on the nearest clock at all times and spoke very little.

In the wake of the death of Maxwell Neuger, the Stop the Nightmare organization announced a Christmas Day memorial service. It was now Monday, the 23rd of December, and Jenny had just thrown out all her Christmas cards.

She went back home, waiting for life to resolve itself. She knew Rich was still in the hospital, but she had yet to go see him. She didn't feel she had the right to involve him further.

She no longer questioned the world; she simply stared out and observed the living lies. Even the Cockroach Woman was beginning to seem apprehensive around her. At night she could hear Captain Daddy and her discussing "their options." Doctors and hospitals seemed the only answer. Captain Daddy agreed but wanted to wait until after the holidays.

Christmas Eve was quiet.

Jenny celebrated the coming of Christmas away from the forced cheerfulness of the others downstairs. She extinguished all of the lights in her room and lit a single candle. Watching the flame flicker, Jenny mourned in silence. When her mourning was ended, she knew she would leave home and everything behind. She had yet to choose her destination, because she still clung to the hope that fate would make the choice for her. Perhaps some bus would jump a curb where she stood waiting, or she would catch pneumonia. Maybe the bombs would explode. Maybe the sky would fall.

At midnight she blew out the candle and dumped the contents of her shoebox into her garbage can, carrying it downstairs and out into the backyard. Everyone else in the house was sleeping. A gentle Christmas flurry was falling outside, but it wasn't enough to snuff the fire she started in the can.

Just before dawn, she began to dress.

She didn't wear black; instead she chose a dark blue jacket and pants with a white shirt. There was a mock formality about it she thought might have amused Max. She left her room neat. If there was a Karma, if circles did bind the universe, then she would do well in the end. If not, whatever. All she wanted was one last bit of truth to take with her.

There was no bus on Christmas, so Jenny walked.

The memorial service was set to begin at ten. Jenny waited on the church steps until the secretary arrived with the keys shortly before nine. Jenny followed her inside and took a seat on one of the hardwood pews. She watched the others arrive.

Jenny was surprised to see she wasn't the only one who thought Max might dislike the overt gestures of a funeral. Very few people wore black. Jenny appreciated that, but she wondered what they were thinking as they filed in. Was Max considered a martyr? Was a martyr necessary for every cause that stumbled along? Jenny remembered asking Max if somebody always had to go to jail for the cause. What was it he had said then? *Sometimes somebody has to do more than that.*

Crazy. Jenny wondered how Reverend Lowell would accept this. She remembered the first STN meeting she attended, and she suspected his words today would be bitter. If the church and meeting halls had been as crowded before Max died, maybe the thugs wouldn't have been so quick to attack. Maybe Max wouldn't have wasted the time that he had occupying jail cells for the cause.

Now Jenny's mind was reeling, and she felt herself slumping in the pew. She was thinking not only about Max, but also about her mother. And the razor in the bathtub. Without at first realizing why, Jenny felt hot tears begin to stream down her cheeks. What was this?

It was a razor in the bathtub.

Jenny was giggling, laughing, when she found her mother in the bathtub. She was playing in her room when she heard the sounds in the hall. Gurgling, wet noises. Lieutenant Daddy was in the missile field, and they were living in base housing at Ellsworth Air Force Base, in Rapid City, South Dakota. Jenny went into the hall and saw water coming from beneath the bathroom door. It was puddling into the hall, and the faucets were still gushing inside. Immediately, Jenny realized what had happened. Mom had started the water for a bath, then went downstairs for something and got sidetracked. The tub inside the bathroom must be overflowing. Calling downstairs to Mom, Jenny ran into the bathroom to stop the water—

But there was a razor in the bathtub.

The image was still vivid after these years, but Jenny hadn't really seen anything then. Mom had turned on the bathwater, and her wounds were under the rising tide. Sloshing water mixed with streams of red, ran over the side of the basin. Mom's eyes were open, but she didn't answer Jenny's screams. She just stared ahead at the wall. Floating in the soap dish, clattering against the side of the tub, was Lieutenant Daddy's straight razor.

Jenny felt a hand on her shoulder. She turned to see

183

a big man with fat cheeks. He swallowed and nodded at her. "He was a good man."

Jenny blinked. He was a good man? Mom liked to dance in the rain. And when they took her out of the house on the gurney, Lieutenant Daddy had to hold Jenny back as she screamed, "Where are you taking her?"

Where were they taking Max?

Jenny choked, sniffing back the tears. What was this feeling called? Acceptance? If she could have found the strength to speak, Jenny knew what her final words would be:

Death is too final and too common to use as a weapon for or against any cause. Max's death wasn't a sacrifice. It was a tragedy. And a waste.

Jenny waited.

After a time the crowd quieted, and Reverend Lowell mounted the podium and spoke. "I will not start this service, as is usually my pleasure to do each year, by saying 'Merry Christmas.' I do this not to detract from the feeling of joy at the birth of Christ that I know we are all feeling, but as a gesture to a man I considered a friend: Maxwell David Neuger."

Jenny tried to choke back the tears and listen.

Reverend Lowell continued. "Max was twenty-four years old. His next birthday was at the end of August, but Max knew when he came to us that he wasn't going to see that birthday. Max had leukemia."

The silence deadened, if such a thing was possible. Jenny tensed. What was he saying? What was he doing?

"Max's story isn't a story of death; it's a story of life, hope, and sacrifice. All of us look forward to long, full lives, but how much time are we willing to give to others? Max knew his time was short. He could have spent his last days on the beach, at a party, but he didn't. He chose to devote himself to a cause—the cause of peace and a nuclear-free world. How do I speak about this sort of sacrifice?"

Jenny chilled. Sacrifice? There was no sacrifice, only tragedy and acceptance. Then you had to go on. Mom was a tragedy, and now it was time for acceptance. Max was a tragedy. How long would it take before anyone accepted that?

Reverend Lowell spoke now very slowly. "How far are we each, individually, willing to give of ourselves in order to help those around us? Max never had to ask that question."

Jenny held her breath a second, then released it. Was all this what it appeared to be? She felt her mind pulling, trying to tear itself away. Maybe there was some reason to it, some truth. Maybe the same would be true about Mom. Jenny had, after all, never seen the wounds. Maybe she hadn't really died that day; maybe she recovered in some hospital—

Reverend Lowell asked the congregation, "How much have we done with our own lives so far? Max never had to ask that question either."

"I'll ask that question."

Reverend Lowell jerked his eyes from the podium. He surveyed the murmuring crowd before him and opened his mouth to speak, but Jenny interrupted him again. "I want to ask the question."

Now there was a definite buzz in the church, and Reverend Lowell looked pained. Jenny stood, her tears an ally now. Her voice was raspy from her silence, and at first she had trouble raising it above a whisper, but she found the strength to speak. If Reverend Lowell wasn't going to address the truth, she would.

Jenny remembered something she had once read: "A misplaced truth has toppled nations, while a well-crafted lie can save men's souls." Perhaps Reverend Lowell agreed with that bent philosophy. Jenny no longer did.

"Was it worth it?" she asked. "Was Max not being alive right now worth any of it?"

Reverend Lowell seemed nervous. "Max's condition . . . He knew that he—"

"A day!" Jenny yelled. "Was Max losing a single day, a single hour, of whatever time he had worth any of this?"

"Sometimes the choices are not ours . . ."

"The choices were ours. You brought him here. You brought Max here to cross your white lines, to climb

185

fences, to go to jail. Because you were afraid to do it yourself. You brought him here to self-destruct right on schedule . . ." Jenny choked, furious with herself. She had to finish. "You brought him here to die in all the newspapers, if he could manage that for you."

Reverend Lowell looked angry now. "Jenny, to think that anyone, even for a minute, considered—"

"That was the problem. None of you, even for a minute, considered."

Reverend Lowell said nothing.

Jenny gasped, taking air. There was one more thing to say. "My mother is dead. She killed herself. I don't like to believe that truth either, but I should. And I'll try. Why don't the rest of you believe the truth now?"

Still Reverend Lowell said nothing.

Jenny left the church.

Twenty-two

The old man in the next bed was asleep. Bored, Rich absent-mindedly changed the channels on the television. The remains of breakfast lay on his tray, shoved rudely aside. There wasn't much in the way of Christmas Day programming on television yet, but when Rich looked down from the set, he saw his father standing in the doorway. Gus was in uniform, his green fatigues with the big stripes. Rich imagined the yellowing newspaper headline: SHARP MISSILE SERGEANT VISITS WOUNDED SON. Finally, Gus asked, "How you doing?"

Rich shrugged. "I'm okay."

Gus stepped into the room. He cleared his throat. "I can't find your doctor. I . . . I wanted to know . . ."

"Cracked ribs," said Rich. "One broken through. I can't walk around for a while, or I might puncture my lung. Oh, my face is smashed a little."

"I saw that."

There was an uncomfortable silence.

"You got everything you need here? You want something to read?"

Rich shook his head, amazed at his father's ability to act like nothing had happened between them. "I'm fine."

"Looks like it hurts."

Rich shrugged.

"Where were you staying?"

Rich switched off the television. "With a friend."

Gus nodded. "It's okay. I wasn't going to ask who."

"Thank you."

"It's in the papers. What happened, I mean. About that Neuger guy."

"His name was Max."

Gus nodded. "I guess he was cut up pretty bad."

Rich shook his head. "That wasn't really what killed him. He had leukemia. He couldn't stop bleeding."

Gus shifted his balance. He seemed embarrassed. "I know he was your friend . . ."

Rich swallowed. "Yeah, but I wasn't his friend. He got killed on account of me."

"Rich . . ." Gus sounded pained.

Rich looked over, feeling tears behind his eyes. "Dad, I killed my friend."

"You didn't . . ."

"If I hadn't tried to fight . . . If we'd left, he'd be here now. He'd be okay."

Gus shook his head. "You listen to me. I don't for a minute believe any of this anti-nuclear peace crap, not for a minute, but I let this thing go too far." He softened his tone. "If you finally found something you believe in enough to fight for, then it must be pretty important to you. And I guess it must have been pretty important to this Neuger guy, too . . . to Max." Gus moved over and sat himself down in the blue plastic chair at the foot of the bed. He was quiet for a long while, and then he said, "I'd like you to come home when you get out of here."

Rich swallowed, in control. "I want to come home."

"I'm sorry about everything that's happened. Sometimes when I get to drinking too much, I get sort of . . ." His voice trailed off.

Rich nodded again. "That's life."

"Your mom fixed your room back up. Put all of your books back on the shelf."

Rich smiled. "Most of them were on the floor in the first place."

Gus rose. "Well, listen, I've got to get out of here. Your mom is probably going nuts. She wanted to come down here herself, right away, but I was still . . ." He grimaced. "Anyway, I didn't want her to come in and find you in traction and mummy bandages."

188

"Neither would I."

"We'll stop by later this evening."

Rich nodded.

Gus started to leave, but he paused at the door. "I just want you to know when I heard the story about what you did, I wasn't mad. I was proud."

Rich swallowed, watching his father leave. He reached back for the remote control and switched on a football game. He lowered the volume on the set and watched until almost three o'clock. That was when Jenny stopped by.

She stood in the doorway, and then she turned and glanced at his sleeping roommate. The old man was hardly ever awake. "Are you all right?" she asked.

"That's my line."

She tried to smile, but it was weak. "I'm fine. I'm sorry I didn't come by before."

"I figured you had reasons."

She reached out and touched the side of his face. Her fingers felt cool there. "Does it hurt?"

"Sheer agony," said Rich. "What about you?"

"I didn't get hurt."

"You know what I mean."

Jenny nodded. "You knew Max was sick, didn't you?"

"Not all the time. After a while I started seeing things. Then . . ."

"Everybody told me he was a junkie."

"I guess he sort of was. But he wasn't addicted to drugs."

Jenny nodded. "Do you know everything?"

Rich tried to smile. "I like to think so. I was thinking about everything, about Max and Stop the Nightmare." He paused and looked at the old man sleeping in the other bed, then imagined Max in his place, wasting away in some hospital somewhere. "At times I think we all helped kill Max, but now I wonder. Maybe we all helped keep him alive."

Jenny didn't say anything at first. Then she asked, "Did you know my mother was dead? Is dead? Has been for a long time?"

"I . . . I wondered."

"I just figured that out today. Isn't that weird?"

Rich swallowed again. "Merry Christmas."

Jenny patted his bandages. "You too."

"Are you in trouble at home?"

"Not really," she said. "What about you? Are you going home?"

"Yeah." Rich hesitated for a moment, then said, "I feel like you're going somewhere. Leaving."

Jenny shrugged. "Have I made your list yet? Your list of problems?"

"What do you think?"

Jenny looked down and then back at Rich. "I think we all have reasons to leave, but usually we stay."

Rich realized it was true. Even for them. Even though Jenny had every reason to leave him there alone, she didn't.

She sat with him, and they talked. As a matter of fact, Jenny stayed with Rich for quite a while.

Robert Hawks grew up in Michigan City, Indiana, but when he was a child his family moved often, and he considers his roots spread as far as Oklahoma, Kansas, and Michigan. Dedicated to extending those roots even farther, he and his wife and their two young daughters have also claimed Great Falls, Montana and Bury St. Edmunds, England as home. This is his second published novel.

Center Stage Summer

Cynthia K. Lukas

Seventeen year old Johanna Culp is threatened with the loss of her college scholarship when she joins her rebellious older sister in speaking out against a proposed nuclear power plant in her community.

ISBN 0-938961-02-0; 157 pp., $4.95 paperback

Cassandra Robbins, Esq.

Pat Costa Viglucci

Cassandra Robbins is a biracial seventeen year old girl adopted at birth by a white family. Her friendship with two boys—one black, one white—precipitates a crisis over who she is and where she fits in.

". . . the novel has strongly nonracist and nonsexist messages . . . sensitive issues are explored with candor."
—ALA Booklist

ISBN 0-93861-01-2; 176 pp., $4.95 paperback

Hiding Places

Lyn Miller-Lachmann

Faced with the choice between military school and suicide, seventeen year old Mark Lambert decides to run away to New York to rebuild his life on his own. Yet this rebel and closet poet is haunted by a past that threatens to destroy the fragile existence he has constructed.

"[a] fine, sensitive and realistic novel . . . Mark Lambert is a real person with whom the reader can connect. And the people he encounters also are real human beings."
—Robert Cormier

ISBN 0-938961-00-4; 206 pp., $4.95 paperback

Stamp Out Sheep Press books are published by Square One Publishers, Inc., an alternative press located in Madison, Wisconsin. Established in July 1985, Square One Publishers and the Stamp Out Sheep Press imprint were created to provide a clear alternative to the formula fiction that dominates the young adult market today. Rather than avoiding controversial and difficult issues, Stamp Out Sheep Press publishes quality fiction that encourages people to think for themselves about the world and their place in it. Current and forthcoming novels deal with friendships among teenagers of different races and cultures, young people who speak out on contemporary political and social issues and who challenge traditional sex role stereotypes and the experiences of teenagers who live in other countries. Teenagers are involved at every stage of the publication of Stamp Out Sheep Press novels, from the reading of manuscripts to the selling of finished books. Manuscripts submitted by teenage authors receive special attention.

Please see order form on reverse side.

You can order Stamp Out Sheep Press books directly from the publisher. Please enclose $4.95 per book and add $1.05 per book for postage and handling. No C.O.D.'s. Checks should be made out to Square One Publishers. Special volume discounts for 6 or more copies are available; please check the appropriate space on the order form for information on volume discount orders. You may photocopy this page if you don't want to rip it out of your book. Please allow up to 6 weeks for shipment.

· ·

Name _____

Address _____

City _____ State _____ Zip _____

Please send me	number of copies	unit price	total
Cassandra Robbins, Esq.		4.95	
Hiding Places		4.95	
Center Stage Summer		4.95	
The Twenty-Six Minutes		4.95	
postage & handling ($1.05 per book)			
Wis. residents add 5% sales tax			
Total enclosed			

☐ I would like to read manuscripts being considered. ☐ I would like to help with publicity. ☐ I am a teenage writer; please send writer's guidelines. ☐ Please send information on volume discounts. ☐ Please keep me informed about future Stamp Out Sheep Press books.

· ·

Mail coupon to: Stamp Out Sheep Press, P.O. Box 4385, Madison, Wisconsin 53711

TSM